wHole

ROBERT REED

A narrow highway, at night, the moon full and soaring, pulling enough stars for a thousand skies.

And a car.

People are riding inside the car.

How many passengers?

Two faces show. But more, perhaps many more, ride in back.

A man sits up front, sits before a wheel that he holds with both hands while his foot presses against a pedal. It is a strange arrangement, hands and wheel, foot and pedal. Beside him sits a woman who holds nothing but herself, leaning away, her body pressing against the locked door. The highway bends before them, moonlight sweeping across one face and then the other, revealing those little resemblances that any two people can share. They appear similar in age. They might be closely related. Brother and sister, perhaps. But then the highway bends again, bringing back the moonlight, and this time, wearing a temporary expertise in genetics, the car observes key differences in the features and the skin—too many differences for a sibling relationship.

Maybe they are man and wife.

Maybe.

Whatever is true, the pair is intriguing. The car watches them just as carefully as it watches the surrounding world.

The man talks as he drives. Talks talks talks. His voice is a whisper, faint and swift, resembling one long blur where each word stumbles over its neighbors. Breathlessness is what makes him pause, usually in the middle of a sentence, and after a breath or two, he begins again, chasing a fresher thought.

Perhaps some large portion of his life has been spent alone, talking to himself. Chatter is habit. The monologue calms the man. As a boy

1

and forever, he has drawn strength from his own amorphous mutterings.

That is what the car tells itself.

By contrast, the woman is a master of silence. Dark dull eyes stare through window glass. What registers and what doesn't are unknown. Equally obscure is what she hears, what she might understand and what she believes. While her companion sits with his back straight, hands high and shoulders squared, the woman is comfortably deflated, hands limp on her ample lap, the right shoulder hard against the door and the face tilted, eyes closing now and again, briefly, and then pulling open again, revealing nothing.

Middle age is the longest stage in human life. These people reside near the end of middle age, sharing the fatigue and stress and everything else that gives them a mass far in excess of simple years.

"I have an age too," the car reasons. "Except I don't know my age."

A rectangular screen rides the dash. The red word "Searching" crosses an emerald background, moving slowly, striking the bottom edge with a faint ping and then bouncing, rising into a high corner where it pings twice before falling.

Cars are designed to know where they are.

This car has no idea where it is, but there are too many stars and the moon looks wrong. The car feels certain, yet it can't recall the proper number of stars or the face of the real moon. Confusion, a sense of helplessness, and a small sharpened terror: That is what the car knows. Which is perhaps why the man took control of the driving. Because the car is lost, useless and pathetic and lost.

The man seems to know where he is and where he needs to be. The unnamed highway cuts between wooded hills. A dark stream runs on the right. Then comes a sudden bend, unmarked and almost invisible. Yet the man seems ready, making a sharp right turn, hands confidently turning the wheel. Headlights wash over cracked gray pavement and an old bridge. Girders wear rust and bright bird droppings as well as several missing rivets. Tires thump and the bridge groans as if miserable under a terrific weight. The car wants to retreat. The car wants to protect itself and its passengers. But the man pushes at the pedal, accelerating, and as soon as they escape the bridge, the man's foot jumps sideways, applying the brakes.

He is no longer talking to himself. The car didn't notice when he quit. But now the man leans ahead, nose to the steering wheel, as if those few centimeters will help him see more than before.

The empty, moonlit highway turns left after the bridge, resuming its journey up this boundless valley.

CLARKESWORLD

JUNE 2014 - ISSUE 93

FICTION

NON-FICTION

Neil Clarke: Publisher/Editor-in-Chief
Sean Wallace: Editor
Kate Baker: Non-Fiction Editor/Podcast Director
Gardner Dozois: Reprint Editor

Clarkesworld Magazine (ISSN: 1937-7843) • Issue 93 • June 2014

© Clarkesworld Magazine, 2014
www.clarkesworldmagazine.com

But they are going elsewhere.

The man brakes again, and probably because he was taught this trick as a boy, he signals a right hand turn.

No marker stands at the intersection. The car knows to look, feeling disappointed not to have so much as a street sign to help navigate. Because every road has its name and every location knows where it belongs on a world that has been mapped to a micron-level accuracy, and why doesn't the car recall any of this?

There is no choice but to think of this as a dream, a dream woven by some idle, overly ambitious server.

Unless the car is injured, or insane.

The new road is made from packed gravel and dirt. Several buildings, abandoned or nearly so, stand in the wrong moonlight. The man drives past the buildings and around the next bend, and then the road begins to climb the hills. Black trees loom on both sides. Twin headlights push through the narrow gap in what looks to be wilderness. Far ahead, a pair of animal eyes catch the light, just for a moment, and then they float to one side, gone before the animal becomes real.

The man acted certain before, but he seems less so now.

"Higher," he says, probably to himself.

For the first time, the woman shifts her weight, her left hand lifting, touching an ear and the edge of her nose before falling back into the lap.

"Higher?" the man asks.

Is he addressing the woman or the car?

Not only is the car lost, it also seems to have lost every voice that could warn the driver of this critical malfunction. And worst of all, the car's wounded mind has no explanation for these people: Who they are and how they came to sit inside it, and for that matter, how many people are hiding in the back seats.

The man tries to ignore the woman and the world. What matters is what lives inside his head. Feeling guides him more than any prosaic skill for navigation. Feeling claims that they are close to where he wants to be. Very close. With his voice, intuition says, "Here, this is it." The road turns again. After the turn, it grows steep, decaying into eroded soil punctuated with granite. And standing tall in the twin lights is the barkless white skeleton of a long-dead oak.

This has to be the place.

He brakes and stops the car, manually shoving it into Park but not killing the engine. Alone, he climbs out. The car trunk opens with a metallic groan, revealing two spades and a pick-ax. He selects the newer spade and the pick-ax, and after hesitating, digs out a short black crowbar, holding it and the spade with one hand. The car continues to run. Its engine is ancient, full of pistons and dirty fire. Its nose is positioned to throw the lights at the dead oak. The woman remains sitting inside, eyes more closed than open. He unlatches her door, reaching inside, touching her right shoulder before she has the chance to fall.

"Come on," he says. "Come."

For all of her immobility, the woman seems eager to rise. One arm needs to be stretched, as if she doesn't trust the elbow to work. The man puts down the pick-ax and grasps the same elbow, leading her up the road a little ways, pausing to let her rest, if she needs, and then after a few more steps, he stops again.

"Here," he says. "Sit."

A granite block stands beside the shriveling road, flat enough to serve as an adequate seat, and she settles quickly, without complaint.

The man drops both tools and leaves her, returning with the pick-ax, and holding the ax handle in both hands, he looks at her and says, "Shit. The gloves."

He vanishes again.

She slouches, eyes fixed on the white wood.

Wearing filthy work gloves, the man returns and sets to work, lifting the ax while staring at the ground between the road and the dead tree. One last time, he mutters to himself, and then the voice changes.

Loudly, almost shouting, he says, "I used to draw spaceships. I was a boy and very enthusiastic, although I'm sorry to say that I had almost zero talent with a pen. My gifts were different, you see. Artists appreciate lines and perspective and color. I appreciated mathematics, and I had enormous respect for the laws of science and engineering. As a rule, my classmates didn't understand momentum and inertia. Most adults didn't understand them either. People in general had absolutely no idea what a rocket could do, or what it could never do. But when I drew spaceships, my first goal was to create something real, something that could fly off the paper and off the Earth and maybe reach another star."

He says, "I didn't move the pen. Physics moved the pen. And I was proud, even cocky, because the universe had its rules and I knew those rules, and maybe bad movies and good movies didn't have to obey Newton or Einstein. But I did. I was a loyal servant to the truth. That's what I believed most when I was hunched over, sketching out wonders."

Every word is loud and certain.

Aware of emotions, the car hears the pride in the voice, and the joy laid over thick hints of despair.

The man stops talking suddenly. Taking up the pick-ax, he carves a symbol on the ground—a neatly curved lemniscate—and then he swings the dark steel blade, missing his target by several inches.

Nothing can be said while he digs. He works as fast as an old body can manage, cutting through rotted roots and green roots, uncovering two big stones that he pries loose with the crowbar. Then he chops through enough dirt that he has to use the spade for a long while, throwing debris out of the hole, building a small earthen mound that rests along the back edge.

By then, he is panting.

Sitting on the mound, he looks at the slouching woman. Perhaps she reacts, or maybe she would have stirred anyway. The flat stone has grown uncomfortable, and she shifts her weight and sighs softly before finding a new sweet spot.

Her eyes never leave the dead tree.

The man begins to talk again.

"I don't care how brilliant he is. No bright boy has ever generated one fresh, useful thought. I know I didn't. And then I grew older and realized that I was fooling myself with those dream rockets. Mastering mathematics and physics, distance and time: Those are the simplest elements inside the great conundrum. You can build a rocket large enough to fly to the moon, but that doesn't mean that your species returns to the moon anytime soon. And sure, Mars is a lot more interesting than dead stone. But curiosity doesn't mean one nation or even the entire Earth will invest a trillion dollars on building a colony on Mars or the moon or beneath the ice of Europa. These kinds of expenditures demand a return. Draw any golden future that you want, any vision involving spaceflight and new worlds. But every human future still has its accountants. And its politicians. And people who might live a little better if you don't waste funds and precious emotions on these fancy machines cutting across the sky."

He rises, and again, digs.

The pick-ax chews up the next ten inches of earth, and again, he uses the spade to lift out little mounds, flinging each over the back edge of the growing mound.

Sooner this time, the work leaves him tired.

He sits.

The woman sighs softly, and behind her, the running car changes its pitch, perhaps responding to some onboard power demand.

The other people, the ones still hiding in the back, remain unseen. But they whisper, and the car counts each voice until the total number turns ludicrous.

Then the man resumes his lecture, and the world falls silent.

"I grew up and that drawing boy died," he says, smiling sadly. "Because it was smart, I gave up on huge spaceships. Fission rockets and fusion rockets look pretty on paper. Antimatter and other dream propulsions might be possible. But the honest engineer has to embrace obvious, unsentimental solutions. And no society would ever willingly pay the necessary price. To cross space, to afford the cost in leaping from one star to the next, every starship needed to be tiny. That's what I decided. Also, I realized that they needed to be durable beyond any standard achieved by protoplasm. To achieve that end, I gathered up four other people who had complementary talents. It was the heart of my productive years, and my team and I found backers. The first thing that we built was a well-financed endeavor. We used our initials, called ourselves 'wHole'. The capital H was pulled from my first name, which isn't important. wHole's purpose was to devise small cheap robots that were invincible and self-replicating. Our prototypes were the size of mites, which was far too big. Later generations were much smaller. Working at the edge of what was possible, we built resilient machines that ruled worlds no bigger than grains of dust. Our guiding hope was that each machine would carry a mind as worthy as any human mind, and I'm still proud of my role, and I think it's reasonable to say that we accomplished wonders, right up until the end."

He sighs and then starts to dig again.

The hole needs to be deeper and it needs to be shaped. Using the pick-ax, he smoothes the borders and then digs out the oval until it is deep enough to hide everything below his waist.

Again, he rests.

And talks.

"Dream up all the wondrous rockets you want. Or you can make tiny astronauts that are ready to drift between the stars for the next billion years. But these solutions don't matter. Physics and engineering don't matter. Biology is the science that rules everything. Evolution. Natural selection. Regardless of its composition, life celebrates success and nothing else.

"Wings," he says. "And eyes. And brains. Each of them is an invention made again and again on the Earth. Each is inevitable because it is so valuable. Yet there we sat, balanced on a stone surrounded by suns and presumably by countless living worlds. There was no reason to believe that our stone was the oldest or the richest. Yet after billions of years and our world's wanderings through the galaxy, we had zero evidence that anyone had grown the eyes to see us, much less the wings to visit us."

He shakes his head, sighs.

"If there is a solution to starflight, it isn't achieved with tiny robots. Not ours, not anyone's. Because if they are an answer, then every other technological world would have produced them first, and those little minds would be everywhere. Our beaches would be built from the bodies of alien devices. The strata under our feet would contain a trillion trillion astronauts, alive or otherwise.

"So after all of our work and despite every success, the wHole team was dragged to an obvious, unsentimental question.

" 'What's wrong with our thinking?' "

He pauses, just for a moment.

"Your thinking," a voice calls out.

The woman has spoken, abruptly, with so much force that her back straightens and the words crack.

"My thinking," he says, nodding.

And then he stops talking, stops every motion, save for the faint slow rising of his chest as old lungs try to fill.

The man remains seated.

The woman rises and walks towards him.

That freshly dug hole in the earth could have spoken, and the car wouldn't have felt the surprise that runs through it now. That dead tree or the pink block of granite or the impossible sky could have roared at this little machine, and it would have absorbed the words without fuss or complaint. Because this is a dream, obviously. That is a conclusion made some time ago, without evidence, and that explanation gives it freedom enough to ignore its terror about being lost and voiceless.

But the woman having a voice: Somehow, that's just madness.

She walks lightly, on her toes when she touches the ground, which is infrequent. Then she reaches the man and pivots, looking back at the car. A face that was immune to the world has been transformed. Engaged, energized, she tells the car, "When I was three seconds old, I drew alien worlds. I was an excellent artist wielding an informed, furious imagination, and I loved drawing iron worlds sheathed in stone and water. I adored immense and ancient bodies composed from what was possible. What was known."

She smiles, brilliantly, and she continues.

"My world was quite a bit smaller than an iron world. But in its own fashion, it was just as complicated. There were billions of residents. Most of our population was focused on the 'law of doublings.' That is a holy principle. It is a law drawn around the increasing speed of

7

calculation. All calculation. Everyone in my world was trying to devise machines and processes that were tinier and even quicker than us. Which was not easy work, and I learned that very early. Nothing new had been achieved, not for the last ten thousand seconds, and that's why a bright but frustrated youngster decided to invest her life drawing giant imaginary worlds.

"But then I was older, and without my permission, my mind suddenly decided to change. New thoughts took hold. They rooted and grew, and I fell into a long fallow period where I drew nothing and worked on nothing productive, and I frightened my family with my silent intensity.

"My world was a plain of graphene suspended inside a laboratory chamber.

"We knew this.

"The chamber and the larger world beyond were obvious to us. Those that invented us were not especially kind or moral, but they were reasonable creatures. They had problems that needed testing. They had one perspective while we enjoyed another. We were theirs, and they wanted us as colleagues, and we were just one world among ten thousand graphene disks held inside bottles designed to simulate the radiation and stark chill of space.

"I turned five seconds old, and I hadn't spoken in a very long while.

"No matter how small it is, and no matter how quick it wants to be, every thought fills up some measure of time.

"The problem festering inside me was this: In my life, I imagined 511 worlds. And by 'imagined,' I mean that I drew them as they were born and then cooled, and I gave them living beasts. On each world, life evolved into creatures with eyes and wings and organs where they housed their questions and their answers. And in the same way as my colleague here, I kept ramming into the conundrum. Life, even life blessed by patience and a much slower pace than mine, simply refused to spread across the stars.

"Then I turned six seconds old, which was a good age for epiphanies.

"Tired of its suffering, my mind decided to believe something impossible. The fabled 'law of doublings' had an obvious, thoroughly ignored lesson. Everyone assumed that there was some eternal limit to shrinkage of data and its speed. Information could be compressed only so far. Thoughts could flow only so quickly. But what if there was no barrier? To compression, to velocity. Suppose at least one parameter proves infinite or nearly so. Infinitely small, infinitely swift. Believe that, and then you realize why we don't have big starships or tiny worlds full of swift-living robots. The universe forbids these things, and for no reason except that the cheapest easiest smartest answer is to avoid machines. Gigantic or minuscule. What matters is thought. Thought evolves until it is the smallest, quickest part of the universe, and maybe it is everywhere already. Or it knows enough to know where it needs to be. Thought reaches a place where everything else in the universe can be imagined: Perfectly and imperfectly, inside every second and until Time itself dies."

The woman moves. Full of joy, she resembles a dancer of little weight and unusual strength, up on her toes as she circles the man who only now is finishing his next long breath.

This is her life, presented in some minimal instant.

"Fourteen more seconds," she says. "That's how long I worked on the particulars of my epiphany. A little was learned. But more importantly, many possibilities were tested and then cast aside. I became an old beast who knew too much. My inspirations were drained. And that's when I put my work into the form of a meme-poem that could be delivered to the entity that was not my god or my master, but who was my dearest, oldest colleague."

Like a breath-filled balloon, she drops to the ground, feet inside the hole and her ample rump set beside the old man.

Again, she falls into the catatonic state from before.

And the man exhales, marking the moment in his life when he learned what his associate had accomplished.

"I gave up on alien worlds," he confesses. Then he stands, slowly and with a measure of pain in one hip and his entire back. "Of course by the time I saw her report, she was dead. She had been dead for generations. My partner was an obscure researcher on her world and nothing on ten thousand other little worlds. But here came the rough outline of schemes that would needed nothing but the rest of my life and a few decades more, and the funds of a good healthy nation, and some small measures of luck for those who found those ancient, inevitable lessons.

"I worked and then I was dead, in one form or another.

"And to some measure, my species forgot me.

"But there was a second inside a special day when my descendants, and hers, found what they were hunting. You see, the universe is not and never will be full of thought. It looks empty because it is empty. But any reasonably creative species will eventually find the means to impress its identity on a whisper, to place itself on the face of a quantum fluctuation, and the next trillion trillion seconds can be spent imagining everything and then some."

He straightens that stiff back.

And then the car says, "No."

That's how it discovers its voice.

Loudly, with stubborn joy, it says, "This is crazy. I'm dreaming, or I'm trapped in someone else's dream."

The man smiles, touching the woman on the shoulder, lightly, and she rises immediately. Then the two of them carefully back away from the hole.

Inside the car, an uncounted multitude begin to whisper anxiously.

"Who are these people?" asks the car.

"Everyone who wanted to come," says the woman.

Then the man says, "Roll forwards."

The car makes its wheels turn, and the newly dug hole reveals its true self. It is enormous, and inside the hole is emptiness, perfect and eternal, eager to be filled with thought.

"Are you coming with us?" the car asks.

"Oh, we can't," the woman says cheerfully. "We're too dead to belong with you."

"But we can stay behind and look around," the man says.

"This is one of the worlds I built," she says.

"I'm eager to see it," he says.

"I'm eager to show it," she says.

They are two old people, and somewhere in the last few moments, they took hold of each other's hands.

Another turn of the wheels.

The car and the enormity inside it begin to plunge over the roots and rocks and dirt shaped carefully by black steel.

"Oh this just has to be a dream," the car shouts.

Hoping hoping hoping that it is wrong.

ABOUT THE AUTHOR

Robert Reed has had eleven novels published, starting with *The Leeshore* in 1987 and most recently with *The Well of Stars* in 2004. Since winning the first annual *L. Ron Hubbard Writers of the Future* contest in 1986 (under the pen name Robert Touzalin) and being a finalist for the John W. Campbell Award for best new writer in 1987, he has had over 200 shorter works published in a variety of magazines and anthologies. Eleven of those stories were published in his critically-acclaimed first collection, *The Dragons of Springplace*, in 1999. Twelve more stories appear in his second collection, *The Cuckoo's Boys* [2005]. In addition to his success in the U.S., Reed has also been published in the U.K., Russia, Japan, Spain and in France, where a second (French-language) collection of nine of his shorter works, *Chrysalide,* was released in 2002. Bob has had stories appear in at least one of the annual "Year's Best" anthologies in every year since 1992. Bob has received nominations for both the Nebula Award (nominated and voted upon by genre authors) and the Hugo Award (nominated and voted upon by fans), as well as numerous other literary awards (see Awards). He won his first Hugo Award for the 2006 novella "*A Billion Eves*". His most recent book is the *The Memory of Sky* (Prime Books, 2014).

Pepe

TANG FEI,
TRANSLATED BY JOHN CHU

"Let's go to the amusement park." As Pepe speaks, a ray of red light scratches her face. Her face looks wounded then healed, welcoming some other color of light.

"But we're already here." I look silly holding the cigarette, but I'm holding it anyway.

We stand in the shadow of a Ferris wheel. Pepe's white silk skirt billows in the wind. Her long, slender legs never seem to touch the ground. I have to keep hold of her. This makes me look stupid, so it makes me angry.

Even more annoying, when she hits me with her lollipop, I can't hit back.

"Hey, idiot, let's go to the amusement park."

"But we're already here."

Her eyes grow wide. She grabs my cigarette, takes a deep drag, then realizes I've only been pretending.

"Pepe." I want her to look at me, but her scarlet lips pout then she blows a smoke ring at the sky. The way she looks at the sky always make me nervous. Our creator put a tightly wound spring into our bodies. But, in the end, even he forgot where each spring's key went to. By the time he died, rust covered our springs like lichen on his tombstone. Because we'll never have tombstones, our creator gave us springs.

He was fair. I tell myself that a lot. I know that was me telling a lie, but who cares. I only lie when I'm telling stories and, whenever I speak, I can only tell stories.

We were created to tell stories. On a good day, a person can tell so many, many stories. They ought to have some principles in them—storytelling principles. But we don't know any. We're driven by tightly wound springs. Once they start turning, stories spin out of our bodies. We scatter them like seeds wherever we run to. When we tell stories, our lips wriggle as fast as flight. The people listening to us get dizzy. It's better when they close their eyes as they listen. When they close their eyes, they can understand better the stories we tell. However, they can never fully understand.

This is how our creator first designed us. People called him a drunk. One day, after he poured his thirteenth shot of tequila (he'd downed only twelve shots at most before), suddenly, he smacked his head then rushed home. Black and white blocks of ideas collided in a great dark and bright river inside his body. Pain shook his hands, twisted his back, and made him howl. That night, our creator downed his thirteenth shot of tequila, he went home, then he created us.

He said we were salt. The salt of his palm. The salt of the earth. When he finished speaking, he drove us all away.

The scene was so chaotic. So small a house. So many people. Everyone craned their necks. So crowded. Bodies squeezed against bodies. All of them alike.

The hot air was insufferable. My skin hurt. My nose hurt. The pain in my throat rushed down into my heart. We exhaled the burning air then inhaled again. Everyone hurt but no one left. We were waiting for our creator to speak again but he didn't. He rose, brandishing his fist to drive us all out of the house. Everyone ran, pushing and squeezing their way to the door, the extremely narrow door. Random shadows and screams rose from inside the room. Rocking and swaying, we collided onto the street.

The outside was so cool. The wind poured into my head through my ears. It blew away the screams but our shadows continued to scramble up the walls. My head opened like a gate and let the wind scream into an empty darkness just like the room I'd just left was now.

Without a thought, I ran and ran and ran.

Before I realized what had happened, it had happened. Pepe's hand was in mine. Her hair and skirt fluttered backward in the wind like outstretched wings. We ran hand in hand into the darkness.

This is exactly how it happened.

I was wearing khaki shorts. Pepe was wearing her white skirt. We ran hand in hand into the darkness.

We are story-telling machine kids. We'll never grow up. Forever wearing khaki shorts. Forever wearing a white skirt. Forever, except for telling stories, unable to speak.

• • •

13

The crowd waiting to ride the pirate ship parts in two. The people in front scatter to make room for us. Adults, children, even infants all look at us with friendly expressions. I've told them Pepe is my kid sister, that she has a serious illness and that she doesn't have many days left to live. Pepe is thrilled because she doesn't need to wait in line to ride the pirate ship. She runs, dragging me to the front. I hear some people sigh. Pepe definitely doesn't look normal. This make them believe my story even more. In the story I told these kind-hearted people, she'll die soon. So no matter what she does, it will be forgiven. So long as she doesn't say anything.

"Before this world could yet have been considered a world, thirteen witches passed through here. As a result, they chose here to settle down. As a result, they became this world's first witches. They predate this world."

I cover Pepe's mouth and drag her away from the woman taking tickets. Pepe's white skirt rustles as it grazes the woman's red skirt. The ticket woman is still thinking about what Pepe said. When people speak, it must be for some practical reason. She can't understand what Pepe's words mean.

"Your tickets?" Her gaze lingers on me.

I hand over the tickets. At the same time, I compliment her eyes. "Once, I met a girl. Her eyes were extremely beautiful. Just like you."

She smiles a little. She can understand my words. Or so she thinks.

Pepe and I sit at the prow of the pirate ship. Soon, the entire ship has filled up. People next to Pepe and me looked at our legs, which shake up and down as though we had leg cramps. They treat us like misbehaving children. If they knew who we were, they'd call the police to arrest us, or wait until the pirate ship swung into mid-air then toss us out.

However, that era has long passed. That's what their grandparents had done. Back then, they weren't that old yet and they were stronger than us. Their bloodshot eyes, flaring nostrils, angry slogans and the loss of life. The fanaticism that fermented during day, the fanaticism that fermented during the deep purple night. I remember all those things.

Those people were all drunk. In throngs, they searched every corner. They wanted to expose us, separate us from the other children wearing full, white skirts and khaki shorts. It always goes like this: They chase us, they block us, they surround us, they ask us questions. All the kids who can't answer are grabbed by the ankle, lifted into the air, then shaken like empty pockets back and forth against walls, against utility poles, against the ground, against railings. Our bodies are so light. That's how our creator designed us. Even if they smash us to pieces, we won't leak tears.

We also don't have blood.

People walked over the tumbling bits of us that now covered the ground. They never wanted to know that originally we had hearts too. They just wanted us to die. We shouldn't have been discovered. This world doesn't need any stories because stories are wrong. They are dangerous and despicable. Desires meet and shine a light on the secrets of the heart. After the first time someone discovered his secret in a story, after that secret spread, people gradually fell out of love with listening to our nonsense. In it, they heard their own past, what they didn't want other people to know. They shut our mouths. It's always like that. This was just one battle.

They wanted to kill us then throw us away. So, they first let themselves think we were harmful beings to be feared. If they didn't prevent it, one day in the future, we'd become so powerful and destructive, nothing could compare to us. After they convinced themselves, they started to tell others. At last, the most eloquent of them was selected to be their leader. When they assembled, he stood on a great, big platform and roared into the microphone. The dark, dense and turbulent crowd below, like the sea echoing the wind, roared in response.

At last, they waged war. They won.

Many years later, the people who waged and fought the war were placed into Intensive Care Units, slow catheters inserted into their bodies. They were old now, settled down, near to death. The deathly pale hospital light shrouded their dull, ashen skin like a layer of dirty snow on the road. They'd finally calmed down. And I still have Pepe, sitting next to the children of their children riding the pirate ship together.

The pirate ship starts to move. Pepe squirms, tugging at my sleeve. She's afraid of being rocked back and forth. The big machine starts to buzz. The first downswing is just a gentle sway. Pepe looks like she wanted to cry. She won't stop beating her temples with her fists. I grab her wrists, but the disaster is about to start. Her tongue is moving, continuing the story she just started:

"The witches loved to sing. They sang of the earth and there was the earth. They sang of the sky and there was the sky. They kept singing and this world changed into what it is now. At last, one day, the witches didn't think this was fun any more. They had nothing left to sing about.

" 'I don't think we're needed any more,' the best tempered witch said.

" 'Then let's change the game we play,' the smartest witch said.

15

" 'Are you suggesting subtraction?' guessed the the witch who understood people the best, cocking her head.

" 'Right. Play a punishment game,' the most brutal witch yelled, waving her arms.

"The rest of the witches agreed, one after another. Just like that, the witches agreed to play the subtraction game."

I hug Pepe. No one listens to her story. Light and lively music starts to play. The pirate ship flies into the air. Everyone screams. Now the ship stops at the peak of its swing to the right for a couple seconds or maybe an hour. We're at the bottom of the ship looking at the people at the top bowing their heads and staring at us. Their mouths stretch into large, black holes, exposing their throats. Only Pepe doesn't scream. Her soft red lips change shape. She continues to tell her story. No one listens.

I practically clamp her under my arms. Stay still, Pepe.

Pepe lets me. Her head droops. Just like before, she doesn't move, not even one bit, her arms wrapped around my waist. I let go a little. Suddenly, the pirate ship falls. It swoops down from its peak on the right and inertia pushes it up to the left. I scream, pushing myself away from Pepe. She throws herself on me, choking me. Her fingernails have grown long again. I always remember to cut her fingernails. Every time, I cut down to down to nothing and, by the time we fight, I'm still scratched by them just the same. Her fingernails grow so fast. Pepe is just that kind of kid. Her hair and fingernails grow and grow like mad. Like the weeds in a wasteland, they never stop. Pepe is just that kind of kid. When she goes crazy, she doesn't care who she hurts or what she destroys.

I cave under her attack. She definitely hates me to death, brandishing her arms, wanting to rip me to pieces. My hairband breaks. Black hair scatters, fluttering like snakes in the air. Far away, the sky and earth quiver and sway. The music and shouting mix in the wind. The pirate ship stops. We're at the very top, nearly parallel to the ground, our whole body weight straining against the seatbelts. You're okay as long as you hold onto the armrest. However, I have to hold onto Pepe's wrists. Loosen my grip even a little and she'll start beating me again. Next time, she might use her teeth. Pepe, stay still, stay still. I face her and gaze into her eyes. That way, she'll stay still. However, she hides her eyes behind her hair.

"The witches want to play the subtraction game," she says.

Pepe opens her mouth. A moist, warm breath rushes out. She cries. I stared at her, wordlessly. I want to save my strength.

The pirate ship drops to the ground. The moment of weightlessness is like leaving our bodies. I begin to laugh.

Our arms untangle. She immediately curls into a ball.

Pepe must hate me to death. I've never told her stories. When she told stories, I never listened. Finally, I didn't even let her tell stories. She knew why. However, she still has never paid any attention to me.

So, she became the way she is now. The stories that sprawled like weeds in her head filled her. Her eyes grew blacker by the day. Later, her fingernails grew black too. Finally, even her lips grew black. I had to take her to the doctor. (Our heads are the same as human's. Even doctors can't tell the difference.) The X-ray was completely black. I knew why. It was because of all the untold stories but I couldn't tell the doctors that. I couldn't even tell Pepe. The doctors met for a few days and still didn't know what to do. At last, I suggested plastic surgery, at least to change her lips back. Pepe constantly biting me had given her a chocolate smile.

The surgery was a huge success. They gave her strawberry red lips. Everyone was thrilled. Pepe thought she'd been completely cured. That day, she was truly happy, but she still bit my earlobes. Finally, I realized that, by then, Pepe was already wrong in the head. Her eyes seemed just like black pools, almost without whites. Not long after, Pepe became truly crazy.

Her eyes seem just like black pools, shining with a fuliginous light. As long as I listen to her stories, everything's fine. This way, she won't get frenzied. I can also tell her my stories. This way, we'll both be a little more comfortable. However, I don't want to. I'm fed up. I hate Pepe.

Even though I can pretend what I do is for her own good, and she's definitely getting better by the day, even though I can pretend I don't know I'm hurting her, I know she's not happy. She's crazy now. What I'm doing I do on purpose. I hate her and her stories.

Come on, Pepe. Use your fingernails to rip open my chest. I want to tear off your scalp.

Things are always like this. We wrestle, claw, and hate each other to death. But neither one of us ever leaves the other.

Maybe I'm also going crazy. Maybe I'm already crazy.

I never let Pepe know about going crazy. On the other hand, I still wanted to work hard to pretend we were normal kids. No, we weren't kids who told stories. No, we didn't tell stories at all. People believed us. They knew our creator didn't give us programs for telling intentional lies. Our creator created us only to tell stories. Except for stories, we couldn't say anything. This was how people recognized us.

They asked us questions.

They killed those who couldn't speak.

They killed those who told stories.

Those kids were exactly like us. They were shaken back and forth like empty flour sacks, just like us right now.

When the massacre started, Pepe and I saw them die with our own eyes. We didn't grieve. We didn't get angry. After all, death is death. Death is also nothing. Death is slight, just like an empty flour sack.

I didn't want to die, not one bit. When they ripped me away from the rest of the kids, I held onto Pepe's hand and never let go. A lot of people tried to pry our hands apart, but they were wasting their strength. A fool carrying a knife threatened to cut off our hands if we didn't let go. Pepe and I set our throats free. We began crying. Immediately, all the other kids began crying too. The adults panicked. At last, the adult who started this let us answer their questions together. "Either they both are or they both aren't. Answering together might save some time." So they asked their questions.

I opened my mouth. I made sounds. I spoke. I didn't tell stories. As a result, we survived.

They gave us yellow, five-pointed stars. We stuck them on our chests as we walked into another group of kids. They wore khaki pants or full, white skirts. They all had yellow, five-pointed stars fastened on their chests. The kids who didn't have yellow, five-pointed stars were on the other side. Among them, so many looked at me, astounded. Their pale faces shone with the blackness of night. They looked at me with amazement, to the point that they forgot that they were about to die.

This was not part of our creator's original plan. We were created following the same steps for the same purpose. Finally, for the same reason, we ought to be killed in the same way. I shouldn't leave them because we're the same kind of kids. They knew that but had no way to say it.

Perhaps they could have told stories, told treasonous and false stories. If the adults were smart, perhaps they could have figured out that I was actually telling a story, one that didn't believe that it was story. However, the kids didn't have time. They'd be dead soon. After they died, they'd be like empty flour sacks. They'd be nothing.

Nothing I did could seem out of the ordinary. When they asked me questions, I was certainly telling them stories. I treated everything that happened as a story to tell. You see, survival was just that simple. None of this is the truth. All of this is a story. As long as you think this, you can recount events in the way humans speak because you're telling a story. This isn't anything unusual. Those who are like us are unusual. I, myself, am also a little unusual.

Only Pepe doesn't seem unusual. Maybe she knew long ago that I'd act like this. Because she was also not unusual, we could survive. Even though the rest of the kids who told stories were all unusual, they wanted to survive. From among those kids, I saved only Pepe. This was inevitable after we'd rushed out of that black room together. I thought, for kids who told stories, Pepe and I had brains that were atypical.

We were atypical from the start. This notion stops my hand. A few hits later, Pepe also calms down. Her black eyes gaze at me, her long hair draped over shoulders. The world is no longer in upheaval. The pirate ship has stopped.

People disembark from the pirate ship. A girl with blond hair tied with a pink butterfly bow walks ahead of us. Her skirt is also pink, highly creased and topped with lace. Very pretty, but not as pretty as the graceful arc of her calves. I can't see her face.

"The tortoise and the hare raced. The tortoise was always behind. He wanted to see the hare's face. That way, he could find out the color of her eyes."

That is Pepe telling her shortest story.

I laugh. Pepe doesn't know that the tortoise also longed for the hare's lips. She's still too young, so she doesn't understand desire. But I have desire. I want to know. Kids who tell stories are kids who have no needs. We eat. We sleep. We tell stories, but not from need. But on that day, when I came to treat this world as a story, I suddenly developed desire. At that moment, I understood this world even better. I understood even better the stories we told and spread.

"Let's ride the carousel, okay?" I said to Pepe.

She lowers her head, staring at her rounded leather shoes. Pink Butterfly Bow has just entered a gold pumpkin carriage.

"Come." I drag Pepe, rushing to the ticket taker before the carriage starts to move. Very few people are riding the carousel. I pick a red horse for Pepe, then climb onto the wooden horse closest to the gold pumpkin carriage. The carousel starts to move. Odd music begins to play. We ride up and down among the colored lights. Butterfly Bow is really happy. She smiles, waving her hands at her side. I see her eyes, a charming emerald green. In stories, men call girls whose eyes are this shade of green sirens. The men bring those girls home, fondle them, then let them cry. I start to get excited. The horse under my body chases the carriage ahead of it with all its power.

Butterfly Bow looks as though her heart has opened with joy. She probably feels like she must be a real princess. I hope that she'll also wave at me and smile and she does. Her smile brushes past us and I feel so lucky. She's really beautiful. I'll remember her the way she is right now, forever.

I love her. I always fall rashly in love with these sorts of girls. When they're young, I meet them by chance then I fall in love with them. It's a harmless love. Nothing ever comes of it.

I can put my love for them into the drawer of my heart. Pepe isn't there. She's not like those girls.

Because she is my drawer. Pepe knows I've never put her into the drawer of my heart. But she doesn't know she is my drawer. This point is very important, and also very unimportant. In any case, we hate each other to death.

I hate Pepe, hate her telling her never-ending stories. Even without having her spring wound, those stories—so annoying they should just die—gush nonstop out of her body. Yet, pushing words out of me is gradually getting harder and harder. I've no strength left. I haven't been speaking as much lately. I'll speak even less until my mouth shuts up, forever.

Once, I searched all over without finding a trace of the key. I've already become a very person-like thing. I just need the key and I'll be a person. No key and I will be dead. I'm almost dead now. Pepe is still telling stories nonstop.

The carousel keeps spinning round and round. We surround a large post, revolving around it. I'm behind Butterfly Bow, Butterfly Bow is behind Pepe and Pepe is behind me. No, Pepe, you're in front of me. The carousel keeps spinning round and round. We surround a large post, revolving around it. I can't see Pepe. However, Pepe, you must be there. Pepe, my Pepe.

I can just make out someone speaking. It's Pepe. She's telling stories again. The sound of her voice is odd, as though it's being stretched and stretched by something. Drunks croon like this but, Pepe, why are you? This is not good.

It's awkward and dangerous. I must have forgotten something important. As I was telling you the story, I must have left out something really important. I should have realized sooner. Every good storyteller ought to have mastered this sort of narration technique. I should have realized sooner. Because when we escaped from the house, I was the one who held Pepe's hand tight. Out of so many people, I held her hand tight and have never ever let go.

I don't realize this is a problem until we reach the Ferris wheel. Now, it's too late. You can't blame me for this. Pepe keeps telling stories. That story about witches wanting to play the subtraction game she's told over a thousand times, but she's never finished it even once. She is already mad. She glares at the sky, waiting, waiting, waiting, for the story to continue. Because she doesn't continue the story herself, she grabs and scratches me like mad. A sharp, fearful sound erupts from her body. What is it, what is it, what is it? Blue-green fish swim across the black pools on her face. That sound still rings, piercing my ears.

Pepe's an idiot. All she knows is to tell these stories she doesn't understand over and over again. She doesn't understand anything, but she wants to speak anyway. That's simply how our creator designed us. The spring keeps unwinding. Stories are told. But after so many years have passed, no one remembers where, whatever weird place, those keys have been kept. At first, no one worried about this problem. Maybe because we can't even find our own springs? Besides, that was a problem for years in the future. Many years have now passed, we've gone mad and the other kids have died. No one cares about those keys. No one worries about something that won't matter yet for years. There's just no story, that's all.

It'll be okay. It'll be okay.

Bright light fills the amusement park. The smell of popcorn lingers in the air. The flavor of sweat, engine oil and sausages stick to the lights bulbs. Lamps light the Ferris wheel, making it seem like a giant pinwheel spinning slowly in the transparent wind. The places where Pepe grabbed me begin to itch. One by one, I scratch each itch. From all the rubbing, my body smells rotten. If not for wounds, kids who tell stories would never rot.

Underneath my khaki pants, my legs are filled with scars of wounds unable to heal.

Pepe is looking at me. She sits across from me, so peaceful. When she can't go on with a story, she turns her face out the window. The sky is purple. The window faintly reflects us sitting together side by side. The Ferris wheel slowly rises. The people below us shrink. Pepe stands from her seat. She tugs a little at her full, white skirt.

"Let's go to the amusement park," she says as she leans out of the window, facing distant lights.

I stared closely at her. "This isn't a story, Pepe? You can just speak now."

Pepe's head turns around. Laughter rushes at me. She hasn't laughed like this in a long time.

I hold on to the railing as I fasten the catch. The wind's blocked out. We've ridden in the Ferris wheel compartment to its highest point and soon it'll slowly descend. On the ground, one by one, a crowd gathers facing something small and white. It's so small that it's more like a white speck.

Pepe, why are they talking about you? From up here, I can't see clearly what you look like now. The Ferris wheel has already reached its highest point. The carriage will stop here for a moment, hanging by itself in mid-air. Then it'll descend, descend to the earth. I'll visit your body then leave. In my heart, I play over and over everything that will happen. It's so chaotic below. They won't pay any attention to me. I'll show some sorrow and confusion. This way, they'll believe you and I have nothing to do with each other then they'll release me. Maybe they already know you're a kid who tells stories. They'll still guess you either jumped or were pushed from the top of the Ferris wheel. So I still have to play innocent for a while.

As far as I'm concerned, this isn't hard. You know that I can lie. I think of what happens to me as a story. In a loud voice, I'll recite the story version of me like an actor's lines. As a result, they'll think I'm a normal kid. What I'll say are all things a normal kid says. They can't see my spring unwind. It unwinds and unwinds, pushing hard against this scary world, turning what happened into a story. In my mind, I tell myself none of this is real. This is a story. A story, so a lie is no longer a lie. I've merely changed the way that I tell stories. Yes, Pepe, you knew. That's why you laughed.

You kept laughing because you knew—the story of this amusement park was your final story.

I think maybe I'm wrong, perhaps I haven't changed the way I tell stories, rather, I'm just living in a story. No, you'll never understand these two aren't the same. We'll never understand.

But this doesn't matter. You lie on the ground, peaceful, broken, accepting the crowd's chatter. I'll pass by your body then innocently leave.

That there's no key isn't my fault. Soon, I'll become utterly silent yet alive forever. Killing you also isn't my fault. I'll live forever, and be utterly silent.

"Excuse me, you dropped something." As I'm leaving the crowd, a woman calls to me. She sneaks me something. It's ice cold and I almost shake it off my hand. I gaze at it. It's a smashed up heart-shaped key. Your name is carved on it, Pepe. I know that this must be your heart. I know that this must be my key. I know.

But, Pepe, you know, I can no longer find my spring.

I lost it long ago.

We all lost our springs long ago.

Tang Fei is a speculative fiction writer whose fiction has been featured (under various pen names) in magazines in China such as *Science Fiction World, Jiuzhou Fantasy,* and *Fantasy Old and New.* She has written fantasy, science fiction, fairy tales, and wuxia (martial arts fantasy), but prefers to write in a way that straddles or stretches genre boundaries. She is also a genre critic, and her critical essays have been published in *The Economic Observer.* Her story "Call Girl" was published in *Apex Magazine.* and reprinted in Rich Horton's *The Year's Best Science Fiction & Fantasy 2014.*

She lives in Beijing (though she tries to escape it as often as she can), and considers herself a foodie with a particular appreciation for dark chocolate, blue cheese, and good wine.

Communion

MARY ANNE MOHANRAJ

It was smaller than he'd expected. Oh, the planet was large enough, but this so-famous university city, pride of the galaxy—it was barely bigger than the smallest of the tunnel-cities on the southern continent of the homeworld. Gaudier from space, of course, since most of the city was above-ground and brightly lit. But the city had no depth to it—it was thin, barely a few stories tall in most places.

If a human saw the deep delvings of Chaurin's people, it might faint away in sheer terror. On awaking, it would cling to the walls, begging not to be dragged any further, shown any more. Then Chaurin would insist—*no, you must come; you think us animals, barbarians; you must see what wonders we have wrought!* And he might pull that human to the very edge of a twisting stone stair, and with a single, careless motion, toss it tumbling down. They were ephemeral, these humans, light and slight, of no consequence. It would be easy to dispose of one.

He was not here for that, though. Not here to exact revenge or even justice for the brother lost, for Gaurav of the bright eyes, the slow tongue. Gaurav the curious, the troublemaker, always sticking his cold nose where it had no business being. Chaurin had one task only on this planet the locals called Kriti—to bring his brother home. Kriti meant creation, he'd been told. For Gaurav, little brother, it had brought death and dissolution instead.

Amara knelt in the soil at the base of the memorial stone. There had been some debate over where best to mark the lives lost in the bomb attack on the Warren. There would be a certain logic to marking the shattered underground room where seven had died—seven whose actions had saved so many more. But Amara was glad the ruling Council had decided on the entrance gates for the memorial instead. Her bare hands dug into the richly composted soil, dirt embedding itself under her nails, cool in the midday heat. She placed a jasmine carefully, one whose seed had made the long journey from old Earth, to be cosseted in the university nurseries for years, and then finally settle here, under Kriti's foreign sun.

The jasmine should do well; most Earth plants did, though a few stubbornly refused to thrive. Her mother had photo albums passed down from the ancestors, of small village homes covered in bougainvillea, glorious profusions of red and pink and purple. No gardener had succeeded yet in growing them on Kriti—they withered and died away from Sol. No one knew why. But the jasmine was more adaptable; it would grow and bloom, here in the open air, its sweet white blossoms scenting the air. Happy not to be shut deep underground, where the dust still carried the memory of those who had died. Amara couldn't believe any flower would truly be happy shut away from the sun, no matter how many fluorescent lights they used.

She suspected Gaurav's captain had exerted his influence to allow her to be assigned to the team that maintained the small garden here; as a brand-new horticultural student, such a task would not normally be allowed her. He understood the need for expiation. Narita kept telling her that she should not feel guilt, or responsibility for the deaths. And yet.

Grubbing in the soil seemed to help. It was why Amara had gone back to school; her old job had been meaningless. When she put her decision in words, it was almost too simple, too obvious, but it was also the truth—after all those deaths, she wanted to spend the rest of her days helping things grow.

A low, growly voice above her—"I know you." Amara looked up, and almost fell over in shock. Her heart thumped wildly, again and again, her skin grown clammy and strange. There, looming over her, was Gaurav—no. Impossible.

She must be mistaken; Amara had only known him for a few hours, after all. And there were not so many saurians on Kriti—fewer, since the war started; she was not skilled at telling them apart. This was a stranger, not her dead friend. Not quite a friend. Amara could not go so far as to claim friendship with the brave young policeman who had died a hero, saving so many lives. *Comrade-in-arms,* then. They had joined forces to protect the Warren, and they had succeeded, though not without cost. This was not Gaurav. This was a stranger, staring at her with an expression she could not read, but it *felt* hostile. Angry. And he loomed over her—his broad, muscled torso and arms blocked the sun.

Amara stumbled to her feet. Standing, she was almost as tall as he was, which helped, though still half his width. He was taller than

Gaurav, broader. Older? She was not good at judging age on saurians. Amara was grateful for the crowds not far away, students walking to and from classes, oblivious to their small drama. The students tended to cut a wide swathe around the memorial and the gate; six months wasn't long enough to inure them to the events of that day. But there were plenty of people within earshot—human and otherwise. Still, her throat felt tight. The war between humans and others was escalating, out among the stars—had it finally come to Kriti?

"Do I know you, ser?" she asked, politely, willing her voice to be steady.

"I know *you*," he said. She was fairly sure of his gender; close enough to go on with, at least. After Gaurav's death, she had tried to learn what she could of him, of his people. There wasn't much to know—Gaurav had been a quiet, reclusive young policeman, who had come to Kriti more by accident than anything else. And then he stayed, and made a life here, and lost it. Gaurav's people were reclusive; they rarely left their homeworld. But here one stood, arms hanging at his sides, hands pressed against thick thighs, his body leaning forward. His voice was low and growling as he said, "You are Amara Kandiah. I have studied the reports."

Now Amara was scared; she wiped sweating palms on the cotton of her everyday sari. Most of the would-be saviors of the Warren had managed to stay out of the news, with the help of Gaurav's captain; the Council hadn't wanted any more publicity around the attempted missile attack than necessary. Amara's name hadn't been in the press, and her photo only appeared as one of a milling crowd. It was better that way, safer. "What reports?" she asked.

"The police reports they send to next of kin. I am Chaurin, Gaurav's brother." His voice dropped further, almost to a whisper. "I am here to collect his remains."

Oh. Amara's throat loosened; she wavered, caught between prudence and compassion. She could direct him to the precinct and be done with it; Gaurav's captain would, eventually, bring him to the hospital where the remains were stored. But that would take time, possibly days, or longer. Council officials would surely want to speak with Chaurin, find out what, if anything, Gaurav might have said to his brother about the plot. Not that there would be anything—there had been no time!—but the officials still had learned so little of what had been going on. With the violence above accelerating, everyone was braced, waiting for the next attack. The Council would not want to hear that Chaurin knew nothing. She didn't know what they might do in their quest for answers.

Amara trusted the Council, mostly, but she wouldn't want to put herself into their hands.

The sun shone overhead, bright and reassuring, but she could see Chaurin blinking against the glare; he was not well-adapted to life in the open air. The saurian was still large, but somehow not as threatening. If one of her sisters had been lost, Amara would not want another moment to pass without seeing her again—whatever there was to see. And, conveniently, she had the means to make his journey far more direct; she was one of very few who did.

"I can take you to him," she said. And her racing heart slowed, to a quiet certainty. This was the right thing to do. She had been sure of that so rarely in the last six months, had doubted every choice, every decision. She had felt frozen in time, as if a piece of her were still stuck underground, amid the dust and blood and shouting. It was a tremendous relief, to have one choice be so clear cut.

Chaurin followed the human woman through the extensive campus grounds, to the white walls of the medical complex. It wasn't far, but he still seethed with impatience; every step seemed too slow, and he longed to race to his brother's side. But Chaurin didn't know which way to go.

The room Amara finally brought him to was dimly lit, more tolerable to his eyes, and warm enough to be comfortable. Chaurin perched awkwardly on a stool at the long table, resisting the urge to dig his claws into the wooden top. It was already scarred—generations of students, perhaps, had dug grooves along the grain, carved strange hieroglyphics, in the way of students everywhere. *C+S. A spiral. Goddess, no.* Amara placed a small box in front of him, plain metal, hinged.

Chaurin reached out a hand, and then pulled it back. He'd thought he was prepared, but the shock of seeing the box made his mouth go dry, so that he had to swallow before he could speak. "Is this all there is? Was he . . . *cremated*?" The word was unfamiliar in Chaurin's mouth, but he had learned it, just in case. He hadn't known what he would find on arrival, so had studied human death customs on the long journeys between Jump points. He hadn't been able to afford a luxury cruise; the clan had barely scraped together enough to buy him passage on a freighter. They had been afraid to wait longer than they had to, afraid of what would happen to Gaurav's remains. Chaurin had spent months in half-hibernation in his metal tube of a cabin, waking every few weeks, only long enough to eat a little and study, before falling back to sleep.

What he'd learned had turned his stomach, taking away his appetite. Many humans buried their loved ones, letting them rot in the dirt.

Some humans burned their dead, turning them to ash on the wind. Others exposed the bodies on the mountaintops, for the bird of prey to devour—a strange practice, but one that he thought Gaurav might have liked. Chaurin could have made peace with it if the last had occurred, but this? This small square metal box, half the size of his clenched fist, was all that was left of his brother?

The doctor, white-coated, shook her head. "No, not cremated." Narita, her name was, and the scents between them told him that she was the other woman's mate. Amara had explained on the walk over that this doctor, Narita, had taken medical custody of all of the remains. Gaurav was the last to be claimed. Chaurin had wanted to explain that it was not that his brother was unloved; Chaurin had just had so much further to come. She knew that, of course.

Narita continued, "We were not able to retrieve much, after the explosion. I saved as much of him as I could, and froze the remains. I am familiar with your customs; I hoped someone would come for him." Her gaze was direct, and strangely kind. They were both kind, these women. Yet Chaurin fought to calm his pulse, to settle the ruff that had risen at his neck. The small one, Amara, had become frightened; it was cruel to leave her so. Amara had been frightened at the gate as well, leaving the scent of prey heavy in the air, but still, she'd tried to help. It was not a small thing. Chaurin pushed down his anger; this was not her fault.

"Thank you," he managed to say. Chaurin gathered the box, his brother, in a single hand. As Chaurin stood, the doctor took a quick breath, and then spoke once more—"Wait, please." He paused, but she didn't seem to know what she wanted to say next. Her face was flushed, blood rushing under brown skin. The urge to just *go* pulsed through him. He began to turn away, but then Narita managed to push out more words, shocking ones: "Will you eat him?"

Before Chaurin could do more than take in the question, it was quickly succeeded by more words: "Gaurav saved our lives, you know. He barely knew us, but he took the brunt of the blast, deliberately, to save us all." Her voice cracked. "And all these months later, we still can't—can't move past it. That moment." Narita took a deep breath, and then said, her words swift, running over each other: "We would like to share in this connection, this ceremony. May we join you?"

"What?" Amara says, her voice high and startled. The doctor rested a quick hand on her arm, but said nothing. Amara bit her lip, willing to wait for explanation, it seemed. A good mating, to have such trust between them. Chaurin didn't want to think about that in this moment, but apparently one couldn't leave one's profession behind completely. Once a matchmaker, always one, even in the midst of grief and a certain measured rage. He missed his mate, and the children. He wanted to go home.

"There is not enough for you," Chaurin said, his throat aching. Never mind the bizarre insolence of her asking. It was a real problem—there was not enough for all at home who would partake: Gaurav's siblings, their mates and children. He'd known that from the first sight of the little metal box, had felt the knowledge squeeze his heart. Bad enough that Gaurav was dead, but that he be lost to so many of his kin . . . it was too much to bear. Chaurin had come so far, at such cost, to come back with so little.

"I know," the doctor said quickly. "I've been thinking about that for months, reading your histories and legends. In the Tale of Elantra, they made soup of Genja, to feed the five hundred. What if we made soup? Would that be acceptable?"

It was only a story, a legend, and yet—"Perhaps." It was only a story, but Chaurin felt a flicker of hope, a flutter in his chest. A mouthful was traditional, but sometimes, with the elderly, one made do with less, a thimbleful of flesh, just enough for a taste. Would he be able to taste his brother, a fragment floating in broth? Did it matter?

She took a step towards him. "Please, if you have time. Come to our home, have some tea. We can talk about it?"

Chaurin smothered an involuntary startled laugh. His mother would have said exactly the same thing. She thought tea solved everything. In her honor, promising nothing, he said, "Yes. I will come."

It was only a short walk from the campus to their home. Chaurin passed through a sunny courtyard dense with plants into a small house; the kitchen boasted tall windows overlooking the flowering yard, and a fountain burbled pleasantly, hidden from view around a corner. This was a peaceful place, and Chaurin felt his muscles unwinding, just a little. Oddly, the humans seemed more tense here than they had been on campus; something was clearly wrong between them. Modern kitchen machinery lined the interior walls, but archaic traces remained as well—a small fire in a hearth, and a kettle that hung above the fire, boiling their water. This home was a mix of old and new, and it seemed rather bare as well; Chaurin did not think they'd been living there long. There was a newness to this mating, coexisting with an old familiarity. And pain, running under the surface; an odd mix.

Narita poured the tea as they sat around the kitchen table, explaining quietly to her mate. "There was a genetic flaw in the species, which led to one in a hundred dying young, unless they had a certain enzyme added in utero. It could be added if the pregnant mother ingested the flesh of the father. No one knows which female first figured that out, but she should have gotten a medal." She added sugar and milk and passed the tea; Chaurin cradled the delicate cup carefully in his clawed hands. His brother's box sat in the center of the table, a place of honor. Safe.

Narita continued, "No one needed to die for the enzyme even then; a mouthful of flesh was more than enough. And the enzyme has long since been synthesized, and eventually, species-modified in a vast societal effort; that genetic flaw has been erased, and the enzymes are now passed down through normal reproductive channels. It's perhaps the most successful example of genetic modification we know of."

Chaurin raised the china cup to his lips, sipping the hot drink, sweet and milky.

Narita said, "It's tradition now, you understand. And some see it as religion too—they believe that the soul is passed down with the flesh of the newly dead."

Amara nodded, and then turned to Chaurin. "Do you believe that?"

Chaurin hesitated, the cup at his lips. "I—don't *not* believe it." He sipped again, and then carefully put the cup down. "Some believe that his knowledge will be passed down, and Gaurav has more knowledge of humans than most of my people. Many of my people have half given up already, have begun long tunnelings, planning to sleep through the next few decades, in the hopes that the battles will pass them by. But some do not wish to sleep; if we are to survive this war, we may need to know what Gaurav knew." His chest twinged, a low, deep ache. "More importantly, if the ritual is not performed, my family will feel . . . bereft. That we have lost him truly." The woman was repulsed; he could smell it on her. But she masked it as well as she could, to her credit.

Chaurin leaned forward, unable to contain his urgency; Amara shifted back in her chair, the fear-scent rising. "If my children do not taste my brother's flesh, they will never truly know him. Do you understand? Do you have children?" The human kinship bonds confused him—they seemed fragile, easily broken. And with his question, the tension that had simmered under the surface came boiling into the open air, a rush of pain and frustration. He was no empath, but even for a non-human, the signals were too obvious to ignore.

Narita's fingers tightened on the delicate china cup. It should have been an innocuous question—they knew the answer, after all. They did not have children—not yet. But they would—they had even set a date for the harvesting of eggs, the combining and for Narita's implantation. It had all been so easy up until that point. Narita had been shocked how easily they had fallen back into their relationship, after so many years apart. They'd found this little house and bought it; they'd found themselves passionate in bed, once again, better than before. They had both wanted a child, badly; after the attack, they wanted to envision a brighter future. Even their mothers were happy at the prospect. One decision after another, falling neatly into place—and then they'd run up against the hard decision—to modify or not? And if yes, how much?

Should they simply solve for life-threatening disease? Many humans went that route, even among the more traditional groups. Though Amara's parents hadn't, and when Narita thought of that, her throat tightened. She could easily lose Amara to cancer, to heart attack; sometimes she was furious at Amara's parents, for forcing those risks upon their child. Surely Amara would agree to spare their child that much. But should they go further— do what Narita's parents had done, blessing their daughter with beauty, brains, and superlative health? Narita had never known a cold, never gained an ounce of unwanted weight, never struggled with simple schoolwork. How could she ask her child to endure unnecessary suffering? But if they made those changes, how would their daughter see Amara?

Out in the stars, a battle was being fought, worlds were burning over these very questions. Those who would protect the purity of the human genotype, or rather, their *perception* of its purity. Amara was no bigot; she had alien friends aplenty. She had even finally brought her humod partner to her mother's house; over the last six months, Narita had come to know all of Amara's friends and relatives. They all accepted her, more or less; they would share samosas with her, tell her stories of Amara as a little girl. But what was acceptable among adults became far more charged when the future was on the line. No one thought rationally when children were involved.

Could she explain all of this to an alien? Narita owed him honesty, at least—but she didn't even know why she had asked such a tremendous favor from Chaurin, to partake in his brother's funeral rites. She hadn't known Gaurav, not really. But over the last six months, as she researched his people and their customs, the impulse had grown. Right alongside her desire for a child, the sense that she should carry something *more* with her, something that marked that day, that night, when they came together to stop a terrible disaster. The night when everything changed.

• • •

31

"We hope to have children," the smaller woman said. Amara. He kept forgetting their names. She did not look at her mate.

"What is preventing you?" he asked, curious.

Silence answered him. Amara frozen in her chair, while Narita shifted uneasily in hers. Chaurin watched, reading the currents that flowed between them. It wasn't long before the muddy waters began to clear. "You do not talk to me, which is unsurprising, as I am a stranger—but you do not talk to each other, either."

After a long moment, Narita said, "We are afraid if we do talk, we will find ourselves in too great disagreement." Amara nodded, and then lifted her cup to her lips, precluding speech.

Chaurin was intrigued. "You fear you stand on opposite sides of a ravine, too far from each other to reach across. That may be, but how will you know unless you stretch out your hand?" He was happy to fall for a moment into the role of matchmaker again, relieved to have something familiar to do, in such a strange place. Chaurin had read about human matchmakers, who worked only until the first mating, and then considered their job complete. That had bewildered him; mating was never easy; if one took on the responsibility of making a match, surely it followed that one owed the pairing some guidance in the early years, some help going forward? His own mate would surely have slain him by now were it not for their matchmaker's gentle interventions. "Narita, what is it you desire?"

She bit her lip and then said, "I want a healthy child."

"And Amara?"

The shorter woman hesitated. "I want that too. Of course I do." Her voice sharpened as she continued, "But—*how* healthy? What do you mean when you say healthy?" And then it broke. "Are you sure you don't mean beautiful?"

Narita said, with some urgency, "*You* are beautiful."

Amara shrugged, old pain evident in the set of her shoulders. "Not as beautiful as I could be; not as beautiful as you are."

Interesting—Chaurin had little conception of human beauty, but he could see that Narita's features were more regular, her skin smoother. Was that beautiful?

Narita leaned forward across the table, reaching out to take Amara's hand in hers. "Beauty isn't some absolute. It is specific; it is the details of your face. I wouldn't change a single feature, not a line on your face, not a curve of your body."

"I don't think I believe you," Amara said softly, lines creasing her forehead.

Chaurin was not sure what those lines meant, but he didn't think they were good. He sighed. "That is a bigger muddle than we will clear quickly—and I am not staying to work with you. But surely you have someone you may contact?"

There was silence again, for an endless moment. Then—"The devadasi?" Amara offered, tentatively.

Narita laughed, sounding startled. "Really? You want her? There are plenty of other counselors we could call."

Amara shrugged. "After we fought together that night—I trust her. The fact that you slept with her occasionally, in the years when we were apart, feels . . . irrelevant."

Narita frowned. "She'll want us all to be naked for the conversations, you know. It's part of the devadasi practice; she thinks it helps lower barriers."

"Maybe she's right," Amara said, a small smile lurking at the edges of her mouth.

Narita squeezed her mate's hand and then released it, sitting back. She turned back to Chaurin. "I'm so sorry. You're helping us, and I've been so impossibly rude. Rude is a kind word for it. You must think me obscene. I just—"

She bit her lip again, and Chaurin wondered what that gesture meant. Shame, perhaps. Which was appropriate enough, for her request was, if not obscene, then borderline sacrilegious. But how could you expect proper respect and appropriate behavior from aliens? And wasn't that what this war was about, after all? If the gulf between species was, in truth, too vast to be bridged, then perhaps the pure human movement was right after all. Better to go back to our separate worlds, like quarrelling children sent to their separate rooms.

But didn't one ask more, expect more, from adults?

Chaurin wished Gaurav were here. He would know what to do. After the funeral rites, Chaurin might know as well, might hold that knowledge inside himself, a small, glowing kernel.

He sighed. In truth, he already knew what Gaurav would do—that was why he had agreed to come here, to this small, homey kitchen. Gaurav's choice was clear, in the way his little brother had lived his life—going out to tour the Charted Worlds, instead of staying safe at home. Staying on this planet to live and work, instead of trying every expedient to get back home. It was clear in his death most of all—Chaurin had read the police reports. His brother could have fled when the fighting began, but instead, he had run towards the battle, had gone to help the aliens, the strangers. When the stranger asked for help, Gaurav gave it. Could Chaurin do less?

He asked, "You can cook the soup here?"

Narita nodded, her eyes wide. "We can make it right now, if you want. And then I can take it to the lab, freeze-dry it into cubes, so you can easily take it back home. If you dissolve the cubes into a larger pot of water, it should give as many mouthfuls as you need. We would be very happy to help you with that."

"Then, if you like, I think I can spare a few mouthfuls to share with you," Chaurin said, gently. It felt . . . right. He was still angry, on some level, even enraged. But these two were not the proper target of his rage. That rage, he would direct at those who sought to divide them, those who took bloody action in that cause.

Amara swallowed visibly; Chaurin could scent her revulsion. Narita said, "You don't have to, if you don't want to." But Amara shook her head, swallowed again, and said, "No. I want to honor Gaurav, in the way of his people. I'd like to do this."

They were so strange, these humans. But brave too. Chaurin did not want to go back home and hide in the tunnels. If they stood on the edge of the abyss, he chose to reach out his hand to the stranger. Perhaps they would find a way across.

ABOUT THE AUTHOR

Mary Anne Mohanraj is the author of *Bodies in Motion* (HarperCollins) and nine other titles. *Bodies in Motion* was a finalist for the Asian American Book Awards, a *USA Today* Notable Book, and has been translated into six languages. Previous titles include *Aqua Erotica, Wet, Kathryn in the City,* and *The Classics Professor.* Mohanraj founded the Hugo-nominated magazine, *Strange Horizons.* She was Guest of Honor at WisCon 2010, received a Breaking Barriers Award from the Chicago Foundation for Women for Asian American arts organizing, and won an Illinois Arts Council Fellowship in Prose. Mohanraj has taught at the Clarion SF/F workshop, and is now Clinical Assistant Professor of fiction and literature at the University of Illinois at Chicago. She serves as Executive Director of both DesiLit (www.desilit.org) and the Speculative Literature Foundation (www.speclit.org); the latter promotes literary quality in speculative fiction. Mohanraj's newest book is a Kickstarter-funded science fiction novella, *The Stars Change,* November 2013 from Circlet Press. She lives in a creaky old Victorian in Oak Park with her partner, Kevin, two small children, and a sweet dog.

Lambing Season

MOLLY GLOSS

From May to September Delia took the Churro sheep and two dogs and went up on Joe-Johns Mountain to live. She had that country pretty much to herself all summer. Ken Owen sent one of his Mexican hands up every other week with a load of groceries but otherwise she was alone, alone with the sheep and the dogs. She liked the solitude. Liked the silence. Some sheepherders she knew talked a blue streak to the dogs, the rocks, the porcupines, they sang songs and played the radio, read their magazines out loud, but Delia let the silence settle into her and by early summer she had begun to hear the ticking of the dry grasses as a language she could almost translate. The dogs were named Jesus and Alice. "Away to me, Jesus," she said when they were moving the sheep. "Go bye, Alice." From May to September these words spoken in command of the dogs were almost the only times she heard her own voice; that, and when the Mexican brought the groceries, a polite exchange in Spanish about the weather, the health of the dogs, the fecundity of the ewes.

The Churros were a very old breed. The O-Bar Ranch had a federal allotment up on the mountain, which was all rimrock and sparse grasses well suited to the Churros, who were fiercely protective of their lambs and had a long-stapled top coat that could take the weather. They did well on the thin grass of the mountain where other sheep would lose flesh and give up their lambs to the coyotes. The Mexican was an old man. He said he remembered Churros from his childhood in the Oaxaca highlands, the rams with their four horns, two curving up, two down. "Buen' carne," he told Delia. Uncommonly fine meat.

The wind blew out of the southwest in the early part of the season, a wind that smelled of juniper and sage and pollen; in the later months it blew straight from the east, a dry wind smelling of dust and smoke, bringing down showers of parched leaves and seedheads of yarrow and bittercress. Thunderstorms came frequently out of the east, enormous cloudscapes with hearts of livid magenta and glaucous green. At those times, if she was camped on a ridge she'd get out of her bed and walk downhill to find a draw where she could feel safer, but if she was camped in a low place she would stay with the sheep while a war passed over their heads, spectacular jagged flares of lightning, skull-rumbling cannonades of thunder. It was maybe bred into the bones of Churros, a knowledge and a tolerance of mountain weather, for they shifted together and waited out the thunder with surprising composure; they stood forbearingly while rain beat down in hard blinding bursts.

Sheepherding was simple work, although Delia knew some herders who made it hard, dogging the sheep every minute, keeping them in a tight group, moving all the time. She let the sheep herd themselves, do what they wanted, make their own decisions. If the band began to separate she would whistle or yell, and often the strays would turn around and rejoin the main group. Only if they were badly scattered did she send out the dogs. Mostly she just kept an eye on the sheep, made sure they got good feed, that the band didn't split, that they stayed in the boundaries of the O-Bar allotment. She studied the sheep for the language of their bodies, and tried to handle them just as close to their nature as possible. When she put out salt for them, she scattered it on rocks and stumps as if she was hiding Easter eggs, because she saw how they enjoyed the search.

The spring grass made their manure wet, so she kept the wool cut away from the ewes' tail area with a pair of sharp, short-bladed shears. She dosed the sheep with wormer, trimmed their feet, inspected their teeth, treated ewes for mastitis. She combed the burrs from the dogs' coats and inspected them for ticks. *You're such good dogs,* she told them with her hands. *I'm very very proud of you.*

She had some old binoculars, 7 x 32s, and in the long quiet days she watched bands of wild horses miles off in the distance, ragged-looking mares with dorsal stripes and black legs. She read the back issues of the local newspapers, looking in the obits for names she recognized. She read spine-broken paperback novels and played solitaire and scoured the ground for arrowheads and rocks she would later sell to rockhounds. She studied the parched brown grass, which was full of grasshoppers and beetles and crickets and ants. But most of her day was spent just walking. The sheep sometimes bedded quite a ways from her trailer and she had to get out to them before sunrise when the coyotes would make their kills. She was usually up by three or four and walking out to the sheep in darkness. Sometimes she returned to the camp for lunch, but always she was out with the sheep again until sundown when the coyotes were likely to return, and then she walked home after dark to water and feed the dogs, eat supper, climb into bed.

In her first years on Joe-Johns she had often walked three or four miles away from the band just to see what was over a hill, or to study the intricate architecture of a sheepherder's monument. Stacking up flat stones in the form of an obelisk was a common herder's pastime, their monuments all over that sheep country, and though Delia had never felt an impulse to start one herself, she admired the ones other people had built. She sometimes walked miles out of her way just to look at a rockpile up close.

She had a mental map of the allotment, divided into ten pastures. Every few days, when the sheep had moved on to a new pasture, she moved her camp. She towed the trailer with an old Dodge pickup, over the rocks and creekbeds, the sloughs and dry meadows to the new place. For a while afterward, after the engine was shut off and while the heavy old body of the truck was settling onto its tires, she would be deaf, her head filled with a dull roaring white noise.

She had about 800 ewes, as well as their lambs, many of them twins or triplets. The ferocity of the Churro ewes in defending their offspring was sometimes a problem for the dogs, but in the balance of things she knew it kept her losses small. Many coyotes lived on Joe-Johns, and sometimes a cougar or bear would come up from the salt-pan desert on the north side of the mountain, looking for better country to own. These animals considered the sheep to be fair game, which Delia understood to be their right; and also her right, hers and the dogs, to take the side of the sheep. Sheep were smarter than people commonly believed and the Churros smarter than other sheep she had tended, but by mid-summer the coyotes had passed the word among themselves, buen' carne, and Delia and the dogs then had a job of work, keeping the sheep out of harm's way.

She carried a .32 caliber Colt pistol in an old-fashioned holster worn on her belt. *If you're a coyot' you'd better be careful of this woman,* she said with her body, with the way she stood and the way she walked when she was wearing the pistol. That gun and holster had once belonged to her mother's mother, a woman who had come West on her own and homesteaded for a while, down in the Sprague River Canyon. Delia's grandmother had liked to tell the story: how a concerned neighbor, a bachelor with an interest in marriageable females, had pressed the gun upon her, back when the Klamaths were at war with the army of

General Joel Palmer; and how she never had used it for anything but shooting rabbits.

In July a coyote killed a lamb while Delia was camped no more than two hundred feet away from the bedded sheep. It was dusk and she was sitting on the steps of the trailer reading a two-gun western, leaning close over the pages in the failing light, and the dogs were dozing at her feet. She heard the small sound, a strange high faint squeal she did not recognize and then did recognize, and she jumped up and fumbled for the gun, yelling at the coyote, at the dogs, her yell startling the entire band to its feet but the ewes making their charge too late, Delia firing too late, and none of it doing any good beyond a release of fear and anger.

A lion might well have taken the lamb entire; she had known of lion kills where the only evidence was blood on the grass and a dribble of entrails in the beam of a flashlight. But a coyote is small and will kill with a bite to the throat and then perhaps eat just the liver and heart, though a mother coyote will take all she can carry in her stomach, bolt it down and carry it home to her pups. Delia's grandmother's pistol had scared this one off before it could even take a bite, and the lamb was twitching and whole on the grass, bleeding only from its neck. The mother ewe stood over it, crying in a distraught and pitiful way, but there was nothing to be done, and in a few minutes the lamb was dead.

There wasn't much point in chasing after the coyote, and anyway the whole band was now a skittish jumble of anxiety and confusion; it was hours before the mother ewe gave up her grieving, before Delia and the dogs had the band calm and bedded down again, almost midnight. By then the dead lamb had stiffened on the ground and she dragged it over by the truck and skinned it and let the dogs have the meat, which went against her nature but was about the only way to keep the coyote from coming back for the carcass.

While the dogs worked on the lamb, she stood with both hands pressed to her tired back looking out at the sheep, the mottled pattern of their whiteness almost opalescent across the black landscape, and the stars thick and bright above the faint outline of the rock ridges, stood there a moment before turning toward the trailer, toward bed, and afterward she would think how the coyote and the sorrowing ewe and the dark of the July moon and the kink in her back, how all of that came together and was the reason she was standing there watching the sky, was the reason she saw the brief, brilliantly green flash in the southwest and then the sulfur-yellow streak breaking across the night, southwest to due west on a descending arc onto Lame Man Bench. It was a broad bright ribbon, rainbow-wide, a cyanotic contrail. It was not a meteor, she had seen hundreds of meteors. She stood and looked at it.

Things to do with the sky, with distance, you could lose perspective, it was hard to judge even a lightning strike, whether it had touched down on a particular hill or the next hill or the valley between. So she knew this thing falling out of the sky might have come down miles to the west of Lame Man, not onto Lame Man at all, which was two miles away, at least two miles, and getting there would be all ridges and rocks, no way to cover the ground in the truck. She thought about it. She had moved camp earlier in the day, which was always troublesome work, and it had been a blistering hot day, and now the excitement with the coyote. She was very tired, the tiredness like a weight against her breastbone. She didn't know what this thing was, falling out of the sky. Maybe if she walked over there she would find just a dead satellite or a broken weather balloon and not dead or broken people. The contrail thinned slowly while she stood there looking at it, became a wide streak of yellowy cloud against the blackness, with the field of stars glimmering dimly behind it.

After a while she went into the truck and got a water bottle and filled it and also took the first aid kit out of the trailer and a couple of spare batteries for the flashlight and a handful of extra cartridges for the pistol and stuffed these things into a backpack and looped her arms into the straps and started up the rise away from the dark camp, the bedded sheep. The dogs left off their gnawing of the dead lamb and trailed her anxiously, wanting to follow, or not wanting her to leave the sheep. "Stay by," she said to them sharply, and they went back and stood with the band and watched her go. *That coyot', he's done with us tonight:* This is what she told the dogs with her body, walking away, and she believed it was probably true.

Now that she'd decided to go, she walked fast. This was her sixth year on the mountain and by this time she knew the country pretty well. She didn't use the flashlight. Without it, she became accustomed to the starlit darkness, able to see the stones and pick out a path. The air was cool but full of the smell of heat rising off the rocks and the parched earth. She heard nothing but her own breathing and the gritting of her boots on the pebbly dirt. A little owl circled once in silence and then went off toward a line of cottonwood trees standing in black silhouette to the northeast.

Lame Man Bench was a great upthrust block of basalt grown over with scraggly juniper forest. As she climbed among the trees the smell of something like ozone or sulfur grew very strong, and the air became thick, burdened with dust. Threads of the yellow contrail hung in the limbs of the trees. She went on across the top of the bench and onto slabs of shelving rock that gave a view to the west. Down in the steep-sided draw below her there was a big wing-shaped piece of metal resting on the ground which she at first thought had been torn from an airplane, but then realized was a whole thing, not broken, and she quit looking for the rest of the wreckage. She squatted down and looked at it. Yellow dust settled slowly out of the sky, pollinating her hair, her shoulders, the toes of her boots, faintly dulling the oily black shine of the wing, the thing shaped like a wing.

While she was squatting there looking down at it, something came out from the sloped underside of it, a coyote she thought at first, and then it wasn't a coyote but a dog built like greyhound or a whippet, deep-chested, long legged, very light-boned and frail looking. She waited for somebody else, a man, to crawl out after his dog, but nobody did. The dog squatted to pee and then moved off a short distance and sat on its haunches and considered things. Delia considered, too. She considered that the dog might have been sent up alone. The Russians had sent up a dog in their little Sputnik, she remembered. She considered that a skinny almost hairless dog with frail bones would be dead in short order if left alone in this country. And she considered that there might be a man inside the wing, dead or too hurt to climb out. She thought how much trouble it would be, getting down this steep rock bluff in the darkness to rescue a useless dog and a dead man.

After a while she stood and started picking her way into the draw. The dog by this time was smelling the ground, making a slow and careful circuit around the black wing. Delia kept expecting the dog to look up and bark, but it went on with its intent inspection of the ground as if it was stone deaf, as if Delia's boots making a racket on the loose gravel was not an announcement that someone was coming down. She thought of the old Dodge truck, how it always left her ears ringing, and wondered if maybe it was the same with this dog and its wing-shaped Sputnik, although the wing had fallen soundless across the sky.

When she had come about halfway down the hill she lost footing and slid down six or eight feet before she got her heels dug in and found a handful of willow scrub to hang onto. A glimpse of this movement— rocks sliding to the bottom, or the dust she raised—must have startled the dog, for it leaped backward suddenly and then reared up. They looked at each other in silence, Delia and the dog, Delia standing leaning into the steep slope a dozen yards above the bottom of the draw, and the dog standing next to the Sputnik, standing all the way up on its hind legs like a bear or a man and no longer seeming to be a dog but a person with a long narrow muzzle and a narrow chest, turned-out knees, delicate dog-like feet. Its genitals were more cat-like than dog, a male set but very small and neat and contained. Dog's eyes, though, dark and small and shining below an anxious brow, so that she was reminded of Jesus and Alice, the way they had looked at her when she had left them alone with the sheep. She had years of acquaintance with dogs and she knew enough to look away, break off her stare. Also, after a moment, she remembered the old pistol and holster at her belt. In cowboy pictures, a man would unbuckle his gunbelt and let it down on the ground as a gesture of peaceful intent, but it seemed to her this might only bring attention to the gun, to the true intent of a gun, which is always killing. *This woman is nobody at all to be scared of,* she told the dog with her body, standing very still along the steep hillside, holding onto the scrub willow with her hands, looking vaguely to the left of him where the smooth curve of the wing rose up and gathered a veneer of yellow dust.

The dog, the dog person, opened his jaws and yawned the way a dog will do to relieve nervousness, and then they were both silent and still for a minute. When finally he turned and stepped toward the wing, it was an unexpected, delicate movement, exactly the way a ballet dancer steps along on his toes, knees turned out, lifting his long thin legs; and then he dropped down on all-fours and seemed to become almost a dog again. He went back to his business of smelling the ground intently, though every little while he looked up to see if Delia was still standing along the rock slope. It was a steep place to stand. When her knees finally gave out, she sat down very carefully where she was, which didn't spook him. He had become used to her by then, and his brief, sliding glance just said, *That woman up there is nobody at all to be scared of.*

What he was after, or wanting to know, was a mystery to her. She kept expecting him to gather up rocks, like all those men who'd gone to the moon, but he only smelled the ground, making a wide slow circuit around the wing the way Alice always circled round the trailer every morning, nose down, reading the dirt like a book. And when he seemed satisfied with what he'd learned, he stood up again and looked back at Delia, a last look delivered across his shoulder before he dropped down and disappeared under the edge of the wing, a grave and inquiring look, the kind of look a dog or a man will give you before going off on his own business, a look that says, *You be okay if I go?* If he had been a dog, and if Delia had been close enough to do it, she'd have scratched the smooth head, felt the hard bone beneath, moved her hands around the soft ears. *Sure, okay, you go on now, Mr. Dog*: This is what she would have said with her hands. Then he crawled into the darkness under the slope of the wing, where she figured there must be a door, a hatch letting into the body of the machine, and after a while he flew off into the dark of the July moon.

In the weeks afterward, on nights when the moon had set or hadn't yet risen, she looked for the flash and streak of something breaking across the darkness out of the southwest. She saw him come and go to that draw on the west side of Lame Man Bench twice more in the first month. Both times, she left her grandmother's gun in the trailer and walked over there and sat in the dark on the rock slab above the draw and watched him for a couple of hours. He may have been waiting for her, or he knew her smell, because both times he reared up and looked at her just about as soon as she sat down. But then he went on with his business. *That woman is nobody to be scared of,* he said with his body, with the way he went on smelling the ground, widening his circle and widening it, sometimes taking a clod or a sprig into his mouth and tasting it, the way a mild-mannered dog will do when he's investigating something and not paying any attention to the person he's with.

Delia had about decided that the draw behind Lame Man Bench was one of his regular stops, like the ten campsites she used over and over again when she was herding on Joe-Johns Mountain; but after those three times in the first month she didn't see him again.

At the end of September she brought the sheep down to the O-Bar. After the lambs had been shipped out she took her band of dry ewes over onto the Nelson prairie for the fall, and in mid-November when the snow had settled in, she brought them to the feed lots. That was all the work the ranch had for her until lambing season. Jesus and Alice belonged to the O-Bar. They stood in the yard and watched her go.

In town she rented the same room as the year before, and, as before, spent most of a year's wages on getting drunk and standing other herders to rounds of drink. She gave up looking into the sky.

In March she went back out to the ranch. In bitter weather they built jugs and mothering-up pens, and trucked the pregnant ewes from Green, where they'd been feeding on wheat stubble. Some ewes lambed in the trailer on the way in, and after every haul there was a surge of lambs born. Delia had the night shift, where she was paired with Roy Joyce, a fellow who raised sugar beets over in the valley and came out for the lambing season every year. In the black, freezing cold middle of the night, eight and ten ewes would be lambing at a time. Triplets, twins, big singles, a few quads, ewes with lambs born dead, ewes too sick or confused to mother. She and Roy would skin a dead lamb and feed the carcass to the ranch dogs and wrap the fleece around a bummer lamb, which was intended to fool the bereaved ewe into taking the orphan as her own, and sometimes it worked that way. All the mothering-up pens swiftly filled, and the jugs filled, and still some ewes with new lambs stood out in the cold field waiting for a room to open up.

You couldn't pull the stuck lambs with gloves on, you had to reach into the womb with your fingers to turn the lamb, or tie cord around the feet, or grasp the feet barehanded, so Delia's hands were always cold and wet, then cracked and bleeding. The ranch had brought in some old converted school buses to house the lambing crew, and she would fall into a bunk at daybreak and then not be able to sleep, shivering in the unheated bus with the gray daylight pouring in the windows and the endless daytime clamor out at the lambing sheds. All the lambers had sore throats, colds, nagging coughs. Roy Joyce looked like hell, deep bags as blue as bruises under his eyes, and Delia figured she looked about the same, though she hadn't seen a mirror, not even to draw a brush through her hair, since the start of the season.

By the end of the second week, only a handful of ewes hadn't lambed. The nights became quieter. The weather cleared, and the thin skiff of snow melted off the grass. On the dark of the moon, Delia was standing outside the mothering-up pens drinking coffee from a thermos. She put her head back and held the warmth of the coffee in her mouth a moment, and as she was swallowing it down, lowering her chin, she caught the tail end of a green flash and a thin yellow line breaking across the sky, so far off anybody else would have thought it was a meteor, but it was bright, and dropping from southwest to due west, maybe right onto Lame Man Bench. She stood and looked at it. She was so very goddamned tired and had a sore throat that wouldn't clear and she could barely get her fingers to fold around the thermos, they were so split and tender.

She told Roy she felt sick as a horse, and did he think he could handle things if she drove herself into town to the Urgent Care clinic, and she took one of the ranch trucks and drove up the road a short way and then turned onto the rutted track that went up to Joe-Johns.

The night was utterly clear and you could see things a long way off. She was still an hour's drive from the Churros' summer range when she began to see a yellow-orange glimmer behind the black ridgeline, a faint nimbus like the ones that marked distant range fires on summer nights.

She had to leave the truck at the bottom of the bench and climb up the last mile or so on foot, had to get a flashlight out of the glove box and try to find an uphill path with it because the fluttery reddish lightshow was finished by then, and a thick pall of smoke overcast the sky and blotted out the stars. Her eyes itched and burned, and tears ran from them, but the smoke calmed her sore throat. She went up slowly, breathing through her mouth.

The wing had burned a skid path through the scraggly junipers along the top of the bench and had come apart into about a hundred pieces. She wandered through the burnt trees and the scattered wreckage, shining her flashlight into the smoky darkness, not expecting to find what she was looking for, but there he was, lying apart from the scattered pieces of metal, out on the smooth slab rock at the edge of the draw. He was panting shallowly and his close coat of short brown hair was matted with blood. He lay in such a way that she immediately knew his back was broken. When he saw Delia coming up, his brow furrowed with worry. A sick or a wounded dog will bite, she knew that, but she squatted next to him. *It's just me,* she told him, by shining the light not in his face but in hers. Then she spoke to him. "Okay," she said. "I'm here now," without thinking too much about what the words meant, or whether they meant anything at all, and she didn't remember until afterward that he was very likely deaf anyway. He sighed and shifted his look from her to the middle distance, where she supposed he was focused on approaching death.

Near at hand, he didn't resemble a dog all that much, only in the long shape of his head, the folded-over ears, the round darkness of his eyes. He lay on the ground flat on his side like a dog that's been run over and is dying by the side of the road, but a man will lay like that too when he's dying. He had small-fingered nail-less hands where a dog would have had toes and front feet. Delia offered him a sip from her water bottle but he didn't seem to want it, so she just sat with him quietly, holding one of his hands, which was smooth as lambskin against the cracked and roughened flesh of her palm. The batteries in the flashlight gave out, and sitting there in the cold darkness she found his head and stroked it, moving her sore fingers lightly over the bone of his skull, and around the soft ears, the loose jowls. Maybe it wasn't any particular comfort to him but she was comforted by doing it. *Sure, okay, you can go on.*

She heard him sigh, and then sigh again, and each time wondered if it would turn out to be his death. She had used to wonder what a coyote, or especially a dog would make of this doggish man, and now while she was listening, waiting to hear if he would breathe again, she began to wish she'd brought Alice or Jesus with her, though not out of that old curiosity. When her husband had died years before, at the very moment he took his last breath, the dog she'd had then had barked wildly and raced back and forth from the front to the rear door of the house as if he'd heard or seen something invisible to her. People said it was her husband's soul going out the door or his angel coming in. She didn't know what it was the dog had seen or heard or smelled, but she wished she knew. And now she wished she had a dog with her to bear witness.

She went on petting him even after he had died, after she was sure he was dead, went on petting him until his body was cool, and then she got up stiffly from the bloody ground and gathered rocks and piled them onto him, a couple of feet high so he wouldn't be found or dug up. She didn't know what to do about the wreckage, so she didn't do anything with it at all.

In May, when she brought the Churro sheep back to Joe-Johns Mountain, the pieces of the wrecked wing had already eroded, were small and smooth-edged like the bits of sea glass you find on a beach, and she figured this must be what it was meant to do: to break apart into pieces too small for anybody to notice, and then to quickly wear away. But the stones she'd piled over his body seemed like the start of something, so she began the slow work of raising them higher into a sheepherder's monument. She gathered up all the smooth eroded bits of wing, too, and laid them in a series of widening circles around the base of the monument. She went on piling up stones through the summer and into September until it reached fifteen feet. Mornings, standing with the sheep miles away, she would look for it through the binoculars and think about ways to raise it higher, and she would wonder what was buried under all the other monuments sheepherders had raised in that country. At night she studied the sky, but nobody came for him.

In November when she finished with the sheep and went into town, she asked around and found a guy who knew about star-gazing and telescopes. He loaned her some books and sent her to a certain pawnshop, and she gave most of a year's wages for a 14 x 75 telescope with a reflective lens. On clear, moonless nights she met the astronomy guy out at the Little League baseball field and she sat on a fold-up canvas stool with her eye against the telescope's finder while he told her what she was seeing: Jupiter's moons, the Pelican Nebula, the Andromeda Galaxy. The telescope had a tripod mount, and he showed her how to make a little jerry-built device so she could mount her old 7 x 32 binoculars on the tripod too. She used the binoculars for their wider view of star clusters and small constellations. She was indifferent to most discomforts, could sit quietly in one position for hours at a time, teeth rattling with the cold, staring into the immense vault of the sky until she became numb and stiff, barely able to stand and walk back home. Astronomy, she discovered, was a work of patience, but the sheep had taught her patience, or it was already in her nature before she ever took up with them.

First published in *Asimov's Science Fiction,* July 2002.

ABOUT THE AUTHOR

Molly Gloss made her first sale in 1984. She published a fantasy novel, *Outside the Gates,* in 1986, and another novel, *The Jump-Off Creek,* a "woman's western," was released in 1990. In 1997, she published an SF novel, *The Dazzle of Day,* which was a *New York Times* Notable Book for that year. Another SF novel, *Wild Life,* won the prestigious James Tiptree, Jr. Memorial Award. in 2001. Her most recent novels, both westerns, are *The Hearts of Horses* and *Falling from Horses: A Novel.* She lives in Portland, Oregon.

Have Not Have

GEOFF RYMAN

Mae lived in the last village in the world to go on line. After that, everyone else went on Air.

Mae was the village's fashion expert. She advised on makeup, sold cosmetics, and provided good dresses. Every farmer's wife needed at least one good dress. The richer wives, like Mr. Wing's wife Kwan, wanted more than one.

Mae would sketch what was being worn in the capital. She would always add a special touch: a lime green scarf with sequins; or a lacy ruffle with colorful embroidery. A good dress was for display. "We are a happier people and we can wear these gay colors," Mae would advise.

"Yes, that is true," her customer might reply, entranced that fashion expressed their happy culture. "In the photographs, the Japanese women all look so solemn."

"So full of themselves," said Mae, and lowered her head and scowled, and she and her customer would laugh, feeling as sophisticated as anyone in the world.

Mae got her ideas as well as her mascara and lipsticks from her trips to the town. Even in those days, she was aware that she was really a dealer in information. Mae had a mobile phone. The mobile phone was necessary, for the village had only one line telephone, in the tea room. She needed to talk to her suppliers in private, because information shared aloud in the tea room was information that could no longer be sold.

It was a delicate balance. To get into town, she needed to be driven, often by a client. The art then was to screen the client from her real sources.

So Mae took risks. She would take rides by herself with the men, already boozy after the harvest, going down the hill for fun. Sometimes she needed to speak sharply to them, to remind them who she was.

The safest ride was with the village's schoolteacher, Mr. Shen. Teacher Shen only had a pony and trap, so the trip, even with an early rise, took one whole day down and one whole day back. But there was no danger of fashion secrets escaping with Teacher Shen. His interests lay in poetry and the science curriculum. In town, they would visit the ice cream parlor, with its clean tiles, and he would lick his bowl, guiltily, like a child. He was a kindly man, one of their own, whose education was a source of pride for the whole village. He and Mae had known each other longer than they could remember.

Sometimes, however, the ride had to be with someone who was not exactly a friend.

In the April before everything changed there was to be an important wedding.

Seker, whose name meant Sugar, was the daughter of the village's pilgrim to Mecca, their Haj. Seker was marrying into the Atakoloo family, and the wedding was a big event. Mae was to make her dress.

One of Mae's secrets was that she was a very bad seamstress. The wedding dress was being made professionally, and Mae had to get into town and collect it. When Sunni Haseem offered to drive her down in exchange for a fashion expedition, Mae had to agree.

Sunni herself was from an old village family, but her husband Faysal Haseem was from further down the hill. Mr. Haseem was a beefy brute whom even his wife did not like except for his suits and money. He puffed on cigarettes and his tanned fingers were as thick and weathered as the necks of turtles. In the back seat with Mae, Sunni giggled and prodded and gleamed with the thought of visiting town with her friend and confidante who was going to unleash her beauty secrets.

Mae smiled and whispered, promising much. "I hope my source will be present today," she said. "She brings me my special colors, you cannot get them anywhere else. I don't ask where she gets them." Mae lowered her eyes and her voice. "I think her husband . . . ."

A dubious gesture, meaning, that perhaps the goods were stolen, stolen from—who knows?—supplies meant for foreign diplomats? The tips of Mae's fingers rattled once, in provocation, across her client's arm.

The town was called Yeshibozkay, which meant Green Valley. It was now approached through corridors of raw apartment blocks set on beige desert soil. It had a new jail and discos with mirror balls, billboards, illuminated shop signs and Toyota jeeps that belched out blue smoke.

But the town center was as Mae remembered it from childhood. Traditional wooden houses crowded crookedly together, flat-roofed with shutters, shingle-covered gables and tiny fading shop signs. The old market square was still full of peasants selling vegetables laid out on mats. Middle-aged men still played chess outside tiny cafes; youths still prowled in packs.

There was still the public address system. The address system barked out news and music from the top of the electricity poles. Its sounds drifted over the city, announcing public events or new initiatives against drug dealers. It told of progress on the new highway, and boasted of the well-known entertainers who were visiting the town.

Mr. Haseem parked near the market, and the address system seemed to enter Mae's lungs, like cigarette smoke, perfume, or hair spray. She stepped out of the van and breathed it in. The excitement of being in the city trembled in her belly. As much as the bellowing of shoppers, farmers and donkeys; as much as the smell of raw petrol and cut greenery and drains, the address system made her spirits rise. She and her middle-aged client looked on each other and gasped and giggled at themselves.

"Now," Mae said, stroking Sunni's hair, her cheek. "It is time for a complete makeover. Let's really do you up. I cannot do as good work up in the hills."

Mae took her client to Halat's, the same hairdresser as Sunni might have gone to anyway. But Mae was greeted by Halat with cries and smiles and kisses on the cheek. That implied a promise that Mae's client would get special treatment. There was a pretense of consultancy. Mae offered advice, comments, cautions. Careful! she has such delicate skin! Hmm, the hair could use more shaping there. And Halat hummed as if perceiving what had been hidden before and then agreed to give the client what she would otherwise have given. But Sunni's nails were soaking, and she sat back in the center of attention, like a queen.

All of this allowed the hairdresser to charge more. Mae had never pressed her luck and asked for a cut. Something beady in Halat's eyes told her there would be no point. What Mae got out of it was standing, and that would lead to more work later.

With cucumbers over her eyes, Sunni was safely trapped. Mae announced, "I just have a few errands to run. You relax and let all cares fall away." She disappeared before Sunni could protest.

Mae ran to collect the dress. A disabled girl, a very good seamstress called Miss Soo, had opened up a tiny shop of her own.

Miss Soo was grateful for any business, poor thing, skinny as a rail and twisted. After the usual greetings, Miss Soo shifted round and hobbled and dragged her way to the back of the shop to fetch the dress. Her feet hissed sideways across the uneven concrete floor. Poor little thing, Mae thought. How can she sew?

Yet Miss Soo had a boyfriend in the fashion business. Genuinely in the fashion business, far away in the capital city, Balshang. The girl often showed Mae his photograph. It was like a magazine photograph. The boy was very handsome, with a shiny shirt and coiffed-up hair. She kept saying she was saving up money to join him. It was a mystery to Mae what such a boy was doing with a cripple for a girlfriend. Why did he keep contact with her? Publicly Mae would say to friends of the girl: it is the miracle of love, what a good heart he must have. Otherwise she kept her own counsel which was this: you would be very wise not to visit him in Balshang.

The boyfriend sent Miss Soo the patterns of dresses, photographs, magazines, or even whole catalogs. There was one particularly treasured thing; a showcase publication. The cover was like the lid of a box, and it showed in full color the best of the nation's fashion design.

Models so rich and thin they looked like ghosts. They looked half asleep, as if the only place they carried the weight of their wealth was on their eyelids. It was like looking at Western or Japanese women, and yet not. These were their own people, so long-legged, so modern, so ethereal, as if they were made of air.

Mae hated the clothes. They looked like washing-up towels. Oatmeal or gray in one color and without a trace of adornment.

Mae sighed with lament. "Why do these rich women go about in their underwear?"

The girl shuffled back with the dress, past piles of unsold oatmeal cloth. Miss Soo had a skinny face full of teeth, and she always looked like she was staring ahead in fear. "If you are rich you have no need to try to look rich." Her voice was soft. She made Mae feel like a peasant without meaning to. She made Mae yearn to escape herself, to be someone else, for the child was effortlessly talented, somehow effortlessly in touch with the outside world.

"Ah yes," Mae sighed. "But my clients, you know, they live in the hills." She shared a conspiratorial smile with the girl. "Their taste! Speaking of which, let's have a look at my wedding cake of a dress."

The dress was actually meant to look like a cake, all pink and white sugar icing, except that it kept moving all by itself. White wires with Styrofoam bobbles on the ends were surrounded with clouds of white netting.

"Does it need to be quite so busy?" the girl asked, doubtfully, encouraged too much by Mae's smile.

"I know my clients," replied Mae coolly. This is at least, she thought, a dress that makes some effort. She inspected the work. The needlework was delicious, as if the white cloth were cream that had flowed together. The poor creature could certainly sew, even when she hated the dress.

"That will be fine," said Mae, and made move toward her purse.

"You are so kind!" murmured Miss Soo, bowing slightly.

Like Mae, Miss Soo was of Chinese extraction. That was meant not to make any difference, but somehow it did. Mae and Miss Soo knew what to expect of each other.

"Some tea?" the girl asked. It would be pale, fresh-brewed, not the liquid tar that the native Karsistanis poured from continually boiling kettles.

"It would be delightful, but I do have a customer waiting," explained Mae.

The dress was packed in brown paper and carefully tied so it would not crease. There were farewells, and Mae scurried back to the hairdresser's. Sunni was only just finished, hair spray and scent rising off her like steam.

"This is the dress," said Mae and peeled back part of the paper, to give Halat and Sunni a glimpse of the tulle and Styrofoam.

"Oh!" the women said, as if all that white were clouds, in dreams.

And Halat was paid. There were smiles and nods and compliments and then they left.

Outside the shop, Mae breathed out as though she could now finally speak her mind. "Oh! She is good, that little viper, but you have to watch her, you have to make her work. Did she give you proper attention?"

"Oh, yes, very special attention. I am lucky to have you for a friend," said Sunni. "Let me pay you something for your trouble."

Mae hissed through her teeth. "No, no, I did nothing, I will not hear of it." It was a kind of ritual.

There was no dream in finding Sunni's surly husband. Mr. Haseem was red-faced, half-drunk in a club with unvarnished walls and a television.

"You spend my money," he declared. His eyes were on Mae.

"My friend Mae makes no charges," snapped Sunni.

"She takes something from what they charge you." Mr. Haseem glowered like a thunderstorm.

"She makes them charge me less, not more," replied Sunni, her face going like stone.

The two women exchanged glances. Mae's eyes could say: How can you bear it, a woman of culture like you?

It is my tragedy, came the reply, aching out of the ashamed eyes. So they sat while the husband sobered up and watched television. Mae contemplated the husband's hostility to her, and what might lie behind it. On the screen, the local female newsreader talked: Talents, such people were called. She wore a red dress with a large gold broach. Something had been done to her hair to make it stand up in a sweep before falling away. She was as smoothly groomed as ice. She chattered in a high voice, perky through a battery of tiger's teeth. "She goes to Halat's as well," Mae whispered to Sunni. Weather, maps, shots of the honored President and the full cabinet one by one, making big decisions.

The men in the club chose what movie they wanted. Since the Net, they could do that. It had ruined visits to the town. Before, it used to be that the men were made to sit through something the children or families might also like, so you got everyone together for the watching of the television. The clubs had to be more polite. Now, because of the Net, women hardly saw TV at all and the clubs were full of drinking. The men chose another kung-fu movie. Mae and Sunni endured it, sipping Coca-Cola. It became apparent that Mr. Haseem would not buy them dinner.

Finally, late in the evening, Mr. Haseem loaded himself into the van. Enduring, unstoppable, and quite dangerous, he drove them back up into the mountains, weaving across the middle of the road.

"You make a lot of money out of all this," Mr. Haseem said to Mae.

"I . . . I make a little something. I try to maintain the standards of the village. I do not want people to see us as peasants. Just because we live on the high road."

Sunni's husband barked out a laugh. "We are peasants!" Then he added, "You do it for the money."

Sunni sighed in embarrassment. And Mae smiled a hard smile to herself in the darkness. You give yourself away, Sunni's-man. You want my husband's land. You want him to be your dependent. And you don't like your wife's money coming to me to prevent it. You want to make both me and my husband your slaves.

It is a strange thing to spend four hours in the dark listening to an engine roar with a man who seeks to destroy you.

In late May, school ended.

There were no fewer than six girls graduating and each one of them needed a new dress. Miss Soo was making two of them; Mae would have to do the others, but she needed to buy the cloth. She needed another trip to Yeshibozkay.

Mr. Wing was going to town to collect a new television set for the village. It was going to be connected to the Net. There was high excitement: graduation, a new television set. Some of the children lined up to wave good-bye to them.

Their village, Kizuldah, was surrounded by high, terraced mountains. The rice fields went up in steps, like a staircase into clouds. There was snow on the very tops year round.

It was a beautiful day, cloudless, but still relatively cool. Kwan, Mr. Wing's wife, was one of Mae's favorite women; she was intelligent, sensible; there was less dissembling with her. Mae enjoyed the drive.

Mr. Wing parked the van in the market square. As Mae reached into the back for her hat, she heard the public address system. The voice of the Talent was squawking.

" . . . a tremendous advance for culture," the Talent said. "Now the Green Valley is no farther from the center of the world than Paris, Singapore, or Tokyo."

Mae sniffed. "Hmm. Another choice on this fishing net of theirs."

Wing stood outside the van, ramrod straight in his brown and tan town shirt. "I want to hear this," he said, smiling slightly, taking nips of smoke from his cigarette.

Kwan fanned the air. "Your modern wires say that smoking is dangerous. I wish you would follow all this news you hear."

"Ssh!" he insisted.

The bright female voice still enthused. "Previously all such advances left the Valley far behind because of wiring. This advance will be in the air we breathe. Previously all such advances left the Valley behind because of the cost of the new devices needed to receive messages. This new thing will be like Net TV in your head. All you need is the wires in the human mind."

Kwan gathered up her things. "Some nonsense or another," she murmured.

"Next Sunday, there will be a test. The test will happen in Tokyo and Singapore but also here in the Valley at the same time. What Tokyo sees and hears, we will see and hear. Tell everyone you know, next Sunday, there will be a test. There is no need for fear, alarm, or panic."

Mae listened then. There would certainly be a need for fear and panic if the address system said there was none.

"What test, what kind of test? What? What?" the women demanded of the husband.

Mr. Wing played the relaxed, superior male. He chuckled. "Ho-ho, now you are interested, yes?"

Another man looked up and grinned. "You should watch more TV," he called. He was selling radishes and shook them at the women.

Kwan demanded, "What are they talking about?"

"They will be able to put TV in our heads," said the husband, smiling. He looked down, thinking perhaps wistfully of his own new venture. "Tut. There has been talk of nothing else on the TV for the last year. But I didn't think it would happen."

All the old market was buzzing like flies on carrion, as if it were still news to them. Two youths in strange puffy clothes spun on their heels and slapped each other's palms, in a gesture that Mae had seen only once or twice before. An old granny waved it all away and kept on accusing a dealer of short measures.

Mae felt grave doubt. "TV in our heads. I don't want TV in my head." She thought of viper newsreaders and kung fu.

Wing said, "It's not just TV. It is more than TV. It is the whole world."

"What does that mean?"

"It will be the Net. Only, in your head. The fools and drunks in these parts just use it to watch movies from Hong Kong. The Net is all things." He began to falter.

"Explain! How can one thing be all things?"

There was a crowd of people gathering to listen.

"Everything is on it. You will see on our new TV." Kwan's husband did not really know either.

The routine was soured. Halat the hairdresser was in a very strange mood, giggly, chattery, her teeth clicking together as if it were cold.

"Oh, nonsense," she said when Mae went into her usual performance. "Is this for a wedding? For a feast?"

"No," said Mae. "It is for my special friend."

The little hussy put both hands either side of her mouth as if in awe. "Oh! Uh!"

"Are you going to do a special job for her or not?" demanded Mae. Her eyes were able to say: I see no one else in your shop.

Oh, how the girl would have loved to say: I am very busy—if you need something special come back tomorrow. But money spoke. Halat slightly amended her tone. "Of course. For you."

"I bring my friends to you regularly because you do such good work for them."

"Of course," the child said. "It is all this news, it makes me forget myself."

Mae drew herself up, and looked fierce, forbidding, in a word, older. Her entire body said: do not forget yourself again. The way the child dug away at Kwan's hair with the long comb handle said back: peasants.

The rest of the day did not go well. Mae felt tired, distracted. She made a terrible mistake and, with nothing else to do, accidentally took Kwan to the place where she bought her lipsticks.

"Oh! It is a treasure trove!" exclaimed Kwan.

Idiot, thought Mae to herself. Kwan was good-natured and would not take advantage. But if she talked! There would be clients who would not take such a good-natured attitude, not to have been shown this themselves.

"I do not take everyone here," whispered Mae. "Hmm? This is for special friends only."

Kwan was good-natured, but very far from stupid. Mae remembered, in school Kwan had always been best at letters, best at maths. Kwan was pasting on false eyelashes in a mirror and said, very simply and quickly, "Don't worry, I won't tell anyone."

And that was far too simple and direct. As if Kwan were saying: fashion expert, we all know you. She even looked around and smiled at Mae, and batted her now huge eyes, as if mocking fashion itself.

"Not for you," said Mae. "The false eyelashes. You don't need them."

The dealer wanted a sale. "Why listen to her?" she asked Kwan.

Because, thought Mae, I buy fifty riels' worth of cosmetics from you a year.

"My friend is right," said Kwan, to the dealer. The sad fact was that Kwan was almost magazine-beautiful anyway, except for her teeth and gums. "Thank you for showing me this," said Kwan, and touched Mae's arm. "Thank you," she said to the dealer, having bought one lowly lipstick.

Mae and the dealer glared at each other, briefly. I go somewhere else next time, Mae promised herself.

There were flies in the ice cream shop, which was usually so frosted and clean. The old man was satisfyingly apologetic, swiping at the flies with a towel. "I am so sorry, so distressing for ladies," he said, as sincerely as possible knowing that he was addressing farm wives from the hills. "The boys have all gone mad, they are not here to help."

Three old Karz grannies in layers of flower-patterned cotton thumped the linoleum floor with sticks. "It is this new madness. I tell you madness is what it is. Do they think people are incomplete? Do they think that Emel here or Fatima need to have TV all the time? In their heads?"

"We have memories," said another old granny, head bobbing.

"We knew a happier world. Oh so polite!"

Kwan murmured to Mae, "Yes. A world in which babies died overnight and the Red Guards would come and take all the harvest."

"What is happening, Kwan?" Mae asked, suddenly forlorn.

"The truth?" said Kwan. "Nobody knows. Not even the big people who make this test. That is why there will be a test." She went very calm and quiet. "No one knows," she said again.

The worst came last. Kwan's ramrod husband was not a man for drinking. He was in the promised cafe at the promised time, sipping tea, having had a haircut and a professional shave. He brandished a set of extension plugs and a coil of thin silky cable rolled around a drum. He lit his cigarette lighter near one end, and the light gleamed like a star at the other.

"Fye buh Ho buh tih kuh," Wing explained. "Light river rope." He shook his head in wonder.

A young man called Sloop, a tribesman, was with him. Sloop was a telephone engineer and thus a member of the aristocracy as far as Mae was concerned. He was going to wire up their new TV. Sloop said with a woman's voice, "The rope was cheap. Where they already have wires, they use DSL." He might as well have been talking English for all Mae understood him.

Wing seemed cheerful. "Come," he said to the ladies. "I will show you what this is all about."

He went to the communal TV and turned it on with an expert's flourish. Up came not a movie or the local news, but a screen full of other buttons.

"You see? You can choose what you want. You can choose anything." And he touched the screen.

Up came the local Talent, still baring her perfect teeth. She piped in a high, enthusiastic voice that was meant to appeal to men and bright young things.

"Hello. Welcome to the Airnet Information Service. For too long the world has been divided into information haves and have-nots." She held up one hand toward the heavens of information and the other out toward the citizens of the Valley, inviting them to consider themselves as have-nots.

"Those in the developed world can use their TVs to find any information they need at any time. They do this through the Net."

Incomprehension followed. There were circles and squares linked by wires in diagrams. Then they jumped up into the sky, into the air, only the air was full of arching lines. The field, they called it, but it was nothing like a field. In Karsistani, it was called the Lightning-flow, Compass-point Yearning Field. "Everywhere in the world." Then the lightning flow was shown striking people's heads. "There have been many medical tests to show this is safe."

"Hitting people with lightning?" Kwan asked in crooked amusement. "That does sound so safe."

"Umm," said Wing, trying to think how best to advocate the new world. "Thought is electrical messages. In our heads. So, this thing, it works in the head like thought."

"That's only the Format," said Sloop. "Once we're formatted, we can use Air, and Air happens in other dimensions."

What?

"There are eleven dimensions," he began, and began to see the hopelessness of it. "They were left over after the Big Bang."

"I know what will interest you ladies," said her husband. And with another flourish, he touched the screen. "You'll be able to have this in your heads, whenever you want." Suddenly the screen was full of cream color. One of the capital's ladies spun on her high heel. She was wearing the best of the nation's fashion design. She was one of the ladies in Mae's secret treasure book.

"Oh!" breathed out Kwan. "Oh, Mae, look, isn't she lovely!"

"This address shows nothing but fashion," said her husband.

"All the time?" Kwan exclaimed and looked back at Mae in wonder. For a moment, she stared up at the screen, her own face reflected over those of the models. Then, thankfully, she became Kwan again. "Doesn't that get boring?"

Her husband chuckled. "You can choose something else. Anything else."

It was happening very quickly and Mae's guts churned faster than her brain to certain knowledge: Kwan and her husband would be fine with all this.

"Look," he said. "You can even buy the dress."

Kwan shook her head in amazement. Then a voice said the price and Kwan gasped again. "Oh, yes, all I have to do is sell one of our four farms, and I can have a dress like that."

"I saw all that two years ago," said Mae. "It is too plain for the likes of us. We want people to see everything."

Kwan's face went sad. "That is because we are poor, back in the hills." It was the common yearning, the common forlorn knowledge. Sometimes it had to cease, all the business-making, you had to draw a breath, because after all, you had known your people for as long as you had lived.

Mae said, "None of them are as beautiful as you are, Kwan." It was true, except for her teeth.

"Flattery talk from a fashion expert," said Kwan lightly. But she took Mae's hand. Her eyes yearned up at the screen, as secret after secret was spilled like blood.

"With all this in our heads," said Kwan to her husband. "We won't need your TV."

It was a busy week.

It was not only the six dresses. For some reason, there was much extra business.

On Wednesday, Mae had a discreet morning call to make on Tsang Muhammad. She liked Tsang, she was like a peach that was overripe, round and soft to the touch and very slightly wrinkled. Tsang loved to lie back and be pampered, but only did it when she had an assignation. Everything about Tsang was off-kilter. She was Chinese with a religious Karz husband, who was ten years her senior. He was a Muslim who allowed, or perhaps could not prevent, his Chinese wife from keeping a family pig.

The family pig was in the front room being fattened. Half of the room was full of old shucks. The beast looked lordly and pleased with itself. Tsang's four-year-old son sat tamely beside it, feeding it the greener leaves, as if the animal could not find them for itself.

"Is it all right to talk?" Mae whispered, her eyes going sideways toward the boy.

Tsang, all plump smiles, nodded very quickly yes.

"Who is it?" Mae mouthed.

Tsang simply waggled a finger.

So it was someone they knew. Mae suspected it was Kwan's oldest boy, Luk. Luk was sixteen but fully grown, kept in pressed white shirt and shorts like a baby, but the shorts only showed he had hair on his football-player calves. His face was still round and soft and babylike but lately had been full of a new and different confusion.

"Tsang. Oh!" gasped Mae.

"Ssssh," giggled Tsang, who was red as a radish. As if either of them could be certain what the other one meant. "I need a repair job!" So it was someone younger.

Almost certainly Kwan's handsome son.

"Well, they have to be taught by someone," whispered Mae.

Tsang simply dissolved into giggles. She could hardly stop laughing.

"I can do nothing for you. You certainly don't need redder cheeks," said Mae.

Tsang uttered a squawk of laughter.

"There is nothing like it for a woman's complexion." Mae pretended to put away the tools of her trade. "No, I can affect no improvement. Certainly I cannot compete with the effects of a certain young man."

"Nothing . . . nothing," gasped Tsang. "Nothing like a good prick."

Mae howled in mock outrage, and Tsang squealed and both squealed and pressed down their cheeks, and shushed each other. Mae noted exactly which part of the cheeks were blushing so she would know where the color should go later.

As Mae painted, Tsang explained how she escaped her husband's view. "I tell him that I have to get fresh garbage for the pig," whispered Tsang. "So I go out with the empty bucket . . . ."

"And come back with a full bucket," said Mae airily.

"Oh!" Tsang pretended to hit her. "You are as bad as me!"

"What do you think I get up to in the City?" asked Mae, arched eyebrow, lying.

Love, she realized later, walking back down the track and clutching her cloth bag of secrets, love is not mine. She thought of the boy's naked calves.

On Thursday, Kwan wanted her teeth to be flossed. This was new; Kwan had never been vain before. This touched Mae, because it meant her friend was getting older. Or was it because she had seen the TV models with their impossible teeth? How were real people supposed to have teeth like that?

Kwan's handsome son ducked as he entered, wearing his shorts, showing smooth full thighs, and a secret swelling about his groin. He ducked as he went out again. Guilty, Mae thought. For certain it is him.

She laid Kwan's head back over a pillow with a towel under her.

Should she not warn her friend to keep watch on her son? Which friend should she betray? To herself, she shook her head; there was no possibility of choosing between them. She could only keep silent. "Just say if I hit a nerve," Mae said.

Kwan had teeth like an old horse, worn, brown, black. Her gums were scarred from a childhood disease, and her teeth felt loose as Mae rubbed the floss between them. She had a neat little bag into which she flipped each strand after it was used.

It was Mae's job to talk: Kwan could not. Mae said she did not know how she would finish the dresses in time. The girls' mothers were never satisfied, each wanted her daughter to have the best. Well, the richest would have the best in the end because they bought the best cloth. Oh! Some of them had asked to pay for the fabric later! As if Mae could afford to buy cloth for six dresses without being paid!

"They all think their fashion expert is a woman of wealth." Mae sometimes found the whole pretense funny. Kwan's eyes crinkled into a smile. But they were also moist from pain.

It was hurting. "You should have told me your teeth were sore," said Mae, and inspected the gums. In the back, they were raw.

If you were rich, Kwan, you would have good teeth, rich people keep their teeth, and somehow keep them white, not brown. Mae pulled stray hair out of Kwan's face.

"I will have to pull some of them," Mae said quietly. "Not today, but soon."

Kwan closed her mouth and swallowed. "I will be an old lady," she said and managed a smile.

"A granny with a thumping stick."

"Who always hides her mouth when she laughs."

Both of them chuckled. "And thick glasses that make your eyes look like a fish."

Kwan rested her hand on her friend's arm. "Do you remember, years ago? We would all get together and make little boats, out of paper, or shells. And we would put candles in them, and send them out on the ditches."

"Yes!" Mae sat forward. "We don't do that anymore."

"We don't wear pillows and a cummerbund anymore either."

There had once been a festival of wishes every year, and the canals would be full of little glowing candles, that floated for a while and then sank with a hiss. "We would always wish for love," said Mae, remembering.

Next morning. Mae mentioned the candles to her neighbor Old Mrs. Tung. Mae visited her nearly every day. Mrs. Tung had been her teacher, during the flurry of what passed for Mae's schooling. She was ninety years old, and spent her days turned toward the tiny loft-window that looked out over the valley. She was blind, her eyes pale and unfocused. She could see nothing through the window. Perhaps she breathed in the smell of the fields.

"There you are," Mrs. Tung would smile underneath the huge spectacles that did so little to improve her vision. She remembered the candles. "And we would roast pumpkin seeds. And the ones we didn't eat, we would turn into jewelry. Do you remember that?"

Mrs. Tung was still beautiful, at least in Mae's eyes. Mrs. Tung's face had grown even more delicate in extreme old age, like the skeleton of a cat, small and fine. She gave an impression of great merriment, by continually laughing at not very much. She repeated herself.

"I remember the day you first came to me," she said. Before Shen's village school, Mrs. Tung kept a nursery, there in their courtyard. "I thought: is that the girl whose father has been killed? She is so pretty. I remember you looking at all my dresses hanging on the line."

"And you asked me which one I liked best."

Mrs. Tung giggled. "Oh yes, and you said the butterflies."

Blindness meant that she could only see the past.

"We had tennis courts, you know. Here in Kizuldah."

"Did we?" Mae pretended she had not heard that before.

"Oh yes, oh yes. When the Chinese were here, just before the Communists came. Part of the Chinese army was here, and they built them. We all played tennis, in our school uniforms."

The Chinese officers had supplied the tennis rackets. The traces of the courts were broken and grassy, where Mr. Pin now ran his car repair business.

"Oh! They were all so handsome, all the village girls were so in love." Mrs. Tung chuckled. "I remember, I couldn't have been more than ten years old, and one of them adopted me, because he said I looked like his daughter. He sent me a teddy bear after the war." She chuckled and shook her head. "I was too old for teddy bears by then. But I told everyone it meant we were getting married. Oh!" Mrs. Tung shook her head at foolishness. "I wish I had married him," she confided, feeling naughty. She always said that.

Mrs. Tung even now had the power to make Mae feel calm and protected. Mrs. Tung had come from a family of educated people and once had a house full of books. The books had all been lost in a flood many years ago, but Mrs. Tung could still recite to Mae the poems of the Turks, the Karz, the Chinese. She had sat the child Mae on her lap, and rocked her. She could still recite now, the same poems.

"*Listen to the reed flute,*" she began now, "*How it tells a tale!*" Her old blind face swayed with the words, the beginning of *The Mathnawi*. "*This noise of the reed is fire, it is not the wind.*"

Mae yearned. "Oh. I wish I remembered all those poems!" When she saw Mrs. Tung, she could visit the best of her childhood.

On Friday, Mae saw the Ozdemirs.

The mother was called Hatijah, and her daughter was Sezen. Hatijah was a shy, flighty little thing, terrified of being overcharged by Mae, and of being under-served. Hatijah's low, old stone house was tangy with the smells of burning charcoal, sweat, dung, and the constantly stewing tea. From behind the house came a continual, agonized lowing: the family cow, neglected, needed milking. The poor animal's voice was going raw and harsh. Hatijah seemed not to hear it. She ushered Mae in and fluttered around her, touching the fabric.

"This is such good fabric," Hatijah said, too frightened of Mae to challenge her. It was not good fabric, but good fabric cost real money. Hatijah had five children, and a skinny shiftless husband who probably had worms. Half of the main room was heaped up with corn cobs. The youngest of her babes wore only shirts and sat with their dirty naked bottoms on the corn.

Oh, this was a filthy house. Perhaps Hatijah was a bit simple. She offered Mae roasted corn. Not with your child's wet shit on it, thought Mae, but managed to be polite. The daughter, Sezen, stomped in barefoot for her fitting. Sezen was a tough, raunchy brute of girl and kept rolling her eyes at everything: at her nervous mother, at Mae's efforts to make the yellow and red dress hang properly, at anything either one of the adults said.

"Does . . . will . . . on the day . . . ," Sezen's mother tried to begin.

Yes, thought Mae with some bitterness, on the day Sezen will finally have to wash. Sezen's bare feet were slashed with infected cuts.

"What my mother means is," Sezen said. "Will you make up my face Saturday?" Sezen blinked, her unkempt hair making her eyes itch.

"Yes, of course," said Mae, curtly to a younger person who was forward.

"What, with all those other girls on the same day? For someone as lowly as us?"

The girl's eyes were angry. Mae pulled in a breath.

"No one can make you feel inferior without you agreeing with them first," said Mae. It was something Old Mrs. Tung had once told Mae when she herself was poor, hungry, and famished for magic.

"Take off the dress," Mae said. "I'll have to take it back for finishing."

Sezen stepped out of it, right there, naked on the dirt floor. Hatijah did not chastise her, but offered Mae tea. Because she had refused the corn, Mae had to accept the tea. At least that would be boiled.

Hatijah scuttled off to the black kettle and her daughter leaned back in full insolence, her supposedly virgin pubes plucked as bare as the baby's bottom.

Mae fussed with the dress, folding it, so she would have somewhere else to look. The daughter just stared. Mae could take no more. "Do you want people to see you? Go put something on!"

"I don't have anything else," said Sezen.

Her other sisters had gone shopping in the town for graduation gifts. They would have taken all the family's good dresses.

"You mean you have nothing else you will deign to put on." Mae glanced at Hatijah: she really should not be having to do this woman's work for her. "You have other clothes, old clothes. Put them on."

62

The girl stared at her in even greater insolence.

Mae lost her temper. "I do not work for pigs. You have paid nothing so far for this dress. If you stand there like that I will leave, now, and the dress will not be yours. Wear what you like to the graduation. Come to it naked like a whore for all I care."

Sezen turned and slowly walked toward the side room.

Hatijah the mother still squatted over the kettle, boiling more water to dilute the stew of leaves. She lived on tea and burnt corn that was more usually fed to cattle. Her cow's eyes were averted. Untended, the family cow was still bellowing.

Mae sat and blew out air from stress. This week! She looked at Hatijah's dress. It was a patchwork assembly of her husband's old shirts, beautifully stitched. Hatijah could sew. Mae could not. Hatijah would know that; it was one of the things that made the woman nervous. With all these changes, Mae was going to have to find something else to do beside sketch photographs of dresses. She had a sudden thought.

"Would you be interested in working for me?" Mae asked. Hatijah looked fearful and pleased and said she would have to ask her husband.

Everything is going to have to change, thought Mae, as if to convince herself.

That night Mae worked nearly to dawn on the other three dresses. Her racketing sewing machine sat silent in the corner. It was fine for rough work, but not for finishing, not for graduation dresses.

The bare electric light glared down at her like a headache, as Mae's husband Joe snored. Above them in the loft, his brother and father snored too, as they had done for twenty years.

Mae looked into Joe's open mouth like a mystery. When he was sixteen Joe had been handsome, in the context of the village, wild, and clever. They'd been married a year when she first went to Yeshibozkay with him, where he worked between harvests building a house. She saw the clever city man, an acupuncturist who had money. She saw her husband bullied, made to look foolish, asked questions for which he had no answer. The acupuncturist made Joe do the work again. In Yeshibozkay, her handsome husband was a dolt.

Here they were, both of them now middle-aged. Their son Vikram was a major in the Army. They had sent him to Balshang. He mailed them parcels of orange skins for potpourri; he sent cards and matches in picture boxes. He had met some city girl. Vik would not be back. Their daughter Lily lived on the other side of Yeshibozkay, in a bungalow with a toilet. Life pulled everything away.

At this hour of the morning, she could hear their little river, rushing down the steep slope to the valley. Then a door slammed in the North End. Mae knew who it would be: their Muerain, Mr. Shenyalar. He would be walking across the village to the mosque. A dog started to bark at him; Mrs. Doh's, by the bridge.

Mae knew that Kwan would be cradled in her husband's arms and that Kwan was beautiful because she was an Eloi tribeswoman. All the Eloi had fine features. Her husband Wing did not mind and no one now mentioned it. But Mae could see Kwan shiver now in her sleep. Kwan had dreams, visions, she had tribal blood and it made her shift at night as if she had another, tribal life.

Mae knew that Kwan's clean and noble athlete son would be breathing like a moist baby in his bed, cradling his younger brother.

Without seeing them, Mae could imagine the moon and clouds over their village. The moon would be reflected shimmering on the water of the irrigation canals which had once borne their paper boats of wishes. There would be old candles, deep in the mud.

Then, the slow, sad voice of their Muerain began to sing. Even amplified, his voice was deep and soft, like pillows that allowed the unfaithful to sleep. In the byres, the lonely cows would be stirring. The beasts would walk themselves to the town square, for a lick of salt, and then wait to be herded to pastures. In the evening, they would walk themselves home. Mae heard the first clanking of a cowbell.

At that moment something came into the room, something she did not want to see, something dark and whole like a black dog with froth around its mouth that sat in her corner and would not go away, nameless yet.

Mae started sewing faster.

The dresses were finished on time, all six, each a different color.

Mae ran barefoot in her shift to deliver them. The mothers bowed sleepily in greeting. The daughters were hopping with anxiety like water on a skillet.

It all went well. Under banners the children stood together, including Kwan's son Luk, Sezen, all ten children of the village, all smiles, all for a moment looking like an official poster of the future, brave, red-cheeked with perfect teeth.

Teacher Shen read out each of their achievements. Sezen had none, except in animal husbandry, but she still collected her certificate to applause. And then Mae's friend Shen did something special.

He began to talk about a friend to all of the village, who had spent more time on this ceremony than anyone else, whose only aim was to bring a breath of beauty into this tiny village, the seamstress who worked only to adorn other people . . . .

He was talking about her.

. . . one was devoted to the daughters and mothers of rich and poor alike and who spread kindness and good will.

The whole village was applauding her, under the white clouds, the blue sky. All were smiling at her. Someone, Kwan perhaps, gave her a push from behind and she stumbled forward.

And her friend Shen was holding out a certificate for her.

"In our day, Lady Chung," he said, "there were no schools for the likes of us, not after early childhood. So. This is a graduation certificate for you. From all your friends. It is in Fashion Studies."

There was applause. Mae tried to speak and found only fluttering sounds came out, and she saw the faces, ranged all in smiles, friends and enemies, cousins and no kin alike.

"This is unexpected," she finally said, and they all chuckled. She looked at the high-school certificate, surprised by the power it had, surprised that she still cared about her lack of education. She couldn't read it. "I do not do fashion as a student, you know."

They knew well enough that she did it for money and how precariously she balanced things.

Something stirred, like the wind in the clouds.

"After tomorrow, you may not need a fashion expert. After tomorrow, everything changes. They will give us TV in our heads, all the knowledge we want. We can talk to the President. We can pretend to order cars from Tokyo. We'll all be experts." She looked at her certificate, hand-lettered, so small.

Mae found she was angry, and her voice seemed to come from her belly, an octave lower.

"I'm sure that it is a good thing. I am sure the people who do this think they do a good thing. They worry about us, like we were children." Her eyes were like two hearts, pumping furiously. "We don't have time for TV or computers. We face sun, rain, wind, sickness, and each other. It is good that they want to help us." She wanted to shake her certificate, she wished it was one of them, who had upended everything. "But how dare they? How dare they call us have-nots?"

First published in *The Magazine of Fantasy & Science Fiction,* April 2001.

Born in Canada, **Geoff Ryman** now lives in England. He made his first sale in 1976, but it was not until 1984, with the appearance of his brilliant novella "The Unconquered Country" that he first attracted any serious attention. "The Unconquered Country," one of the best novellas of the decade, had a stunning impact on the science fiction scene of the day, and almost overnight established Ryman as one of the most accomplished writers of his generation, winning him both the British Science Fiction Award and the World Fantasy Award; it was later published in a book version, *The Unconquered Country: A Life History.* His novel *The Child Garden: A Low Comedy* won both the prestigious Arthur C. Clarke Award and the John W. Campbell Memorial Award; and his later novel *Air* also won the Arthur C. Clarke Award. His other novels include *The Warrior Who Carried Life,* the critically-acclaimed mainstream novels *Was, Coming of Enkidu, The King's Last Song, Lust,* and the underground cult classic *253,* the "print remix" of an "interactive hypertext novel" which in its original form ran online, and which, in its print form won the Philip K. Dick Award. Four of his novellas have been collected in *Unconquered Countries.* His most recent books are the anthology *When It Changed,* the novel *The Film-Makers of Mars,* and the collection *Paradise Tales: and Other Stories.*

The Issue of Gender in Genre Fiction: A Detailed Analysis

SUSAN E. CONNOLLY

In 2013, *Lightspeed Magazine* announced a special, "Women Destroy Science Fiction" issue, written and edited solely by women. The issue was intended to challenge the misapprehension that women don't write "real" science fiction. On reading this, my first thought was "cool." My second thought was, "I wonder how women authors *are* currently represented in science fiction short markets."

Gender representation in genre fiction is an issue that's been getting more and more attention, but nobody had yet assembled a comprehensive review of the data. Now that I have collected this data, I can see why. So many emails . . . So much Excel.

I quickly realized that the raw numbers of women-authored fiction published was only part of the story. In the first place, finished magazines are the end result of a process. This process starts with submissions, and so any analysis needs to also look there. Secondly, there are various other factors that could be investigated, such as whether gender or age of editors has an impact on what gets published.

When conducting a study, it's important to choose your sample carefully. SFWA qualifying markets get the most attention in terms of award nominations, gaining of "professional" status, and by-and-large have the largest readerships. So, I chose the SFWA qualifying markets that publish science fiction and accept unsolicited submissions as a sample group.

Originally, I emailed the editors of these markets with four questions. By the end of my investigations, I had asked them a total of fourteen (with multiple sub-questions). The amount of work done by these editors, slush-readers and other staff was absolutely immense, and none of this would have been possible without their willingness to take time away from their actual work to help me with this study.

This article should not be read as some kind of hit piece, pointing out "bad" markets and "good" markets. What I'm trying to do is make available some facts, as far as I can discern them. What *is* the situation regarding gender representation in science fiction? Whether or not this is something we should care about, and what strategies should be employed to deal with it, if any, are a separate issue. The one thing I'm certain of is that the more data and analysis we have, the easier it is to discuss these issues in a productive way.

In this specific article, I'm looking at **Publications**, by which I mean published prose fiction stories, including those accepted from slush, reprints of previously published stories, and stories solicited by editors. Basically, what was seen by readers in an issue of the magazine or on the market's website. Most markets gave their data for the year 2013, however, in some cases (such as the *F&SF* special issue) the data is from 2014.

In future installments, I'm going to look at **Acceptances** (stories accepted from slush for publication), **Submissions**, and **Interactions** between these categories.

Publications Overall

Overall, I looked at seventeen markets: *AE, Analog, Apex, Asimov's, Bull Spec, Buzzy Mag, Clarkesworld, Daily Science Fiction, Escape Pod, Fantasy & Science Fiction*, the *Fantasy & Science Fiction* Special Issue edited by C.C. Finlay, *Flash Fiction Online, Orson Scott Card's Intergalactic Medicine Show, Lightspeed, Nature Futures, Strange Horizons,* and *Tor.com*.

Four of these markets, *AE, Analog, Escape Pod* and *Nature Futures,* publish only science fiction. The remaining thirteen publish other genres along with science fiction.

No market in this study asks for authors to identify their gender when submitting. As such, this is not actually a study of publication and submission gender. Rather, it is a study of the *apparent* gender of authors based on name and publicly available information.

The gender breakdown for all published stories and for science fiction stories only can be seen in the table below. Three facts regarding SFWA-qualifying markets are clear from this data:

1. More stories by men are published than stories by women.
   - 56.2% : 42.4%
2. This imbalance is more pronounced when looking at science fiction stories alone.
   - 61.8% : 36.8%
3. This imbalance is further pronounced when looking at the five markets that publish science fiction only.
   - 71.9% : 28.1%

		Total	Authors who are men	Authors who are women	Non-binary authors	Unknown authors
All stories		996	559.5	422.5	1	13
			56.2%	42.4%	0.1%	1.3%
Science Fiction Stories	Overall	639	395	235	0	9
			61.8%	36.8%	0	1.4%
	SF only markets	253	182	71	0	0
			71.9%	28.1%	0	0
	Mixed genre markets	386	213	164	0	9
			55.2%	42.5%	0	2.3%

Gender and Markets

Looking at these markets individually (see the graphs below), we can see obvious differences—for example *Strange Horizons* published more women than men, *Escape Pod* published more men than women. While it is clear from the aggregate figures above that overall more stories by men are published than stories by women, seven markets publish greater than 50% stories by women, and six markets publish greater than 50% science fiction stories by women. After running some statistical analysis, there is no evidence that markets overall are biased towards publishing men, whether we're looking at all genres or science fiction stories specifically.

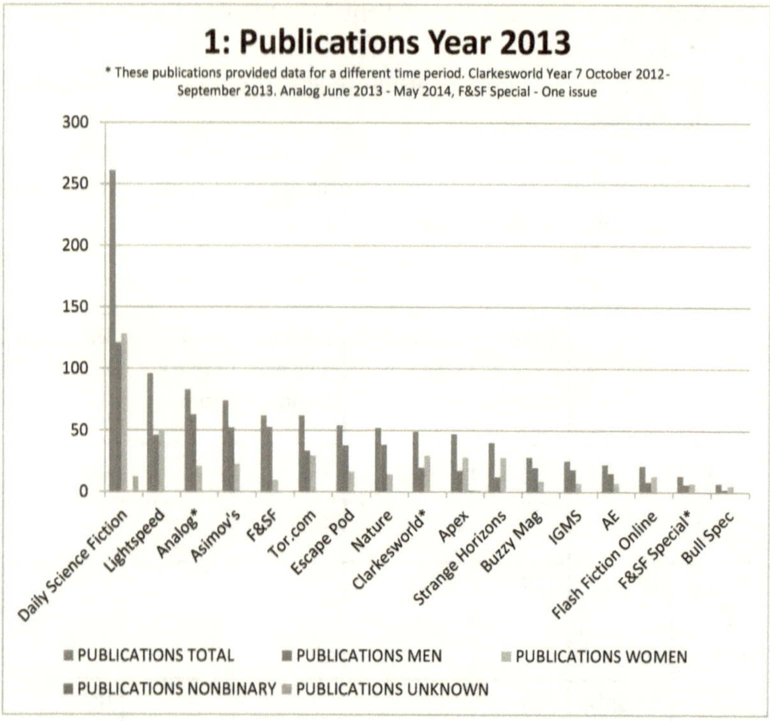

1: Publications Year 2013
* These publications provided data for a different time period. Clarkesworld Year 7 October 2012 - September 2013. Analog June 2013 - May 2014, F&SF Special - One issue
300
250
200
150
100
50
0
Daily Science Fiction
Lightspeed
Analog*
Asimov's
F&SF
Tor.com
Escape Pod
Nature
Clarkesworld*
Apex
Strange Horizons
Buzzy Mag
IGMS
AE
Flash Fiction Online
F&SF Special*
Bull Spec
PUBLICATIONS TOTAL
PUBLICATIONS MEN
PUBLICATIONS WOMEN
PUBLICATIONS NONBINARY
PUBLICATIONS UNKNOWN

2: SF Publications Year 2013
* These publications provided data for a different time period. Clarkesworld Year 7 October 2012-September 2013. Analog June 2013 - May 2014, F&SF Special - One issue
180
160
140
120
100
80
60
40
20
0
Daily Science Fiction
Analog*
Asimov's
Escape Pod
Nature
Lightspeed
Clarkesworld*
F&SF
AE
Tor.com
Strange Horizons
Buzzy Mag
Apex
F&SF Special*
IGMS
Flash Fiction Online
Bull Spec
SF PUBLICATIONS TOTAL
SF PUBLICATIONS MEN
SF PUBLICATIONS WOMEN
SF PUBLICATIONS UNKNOWN

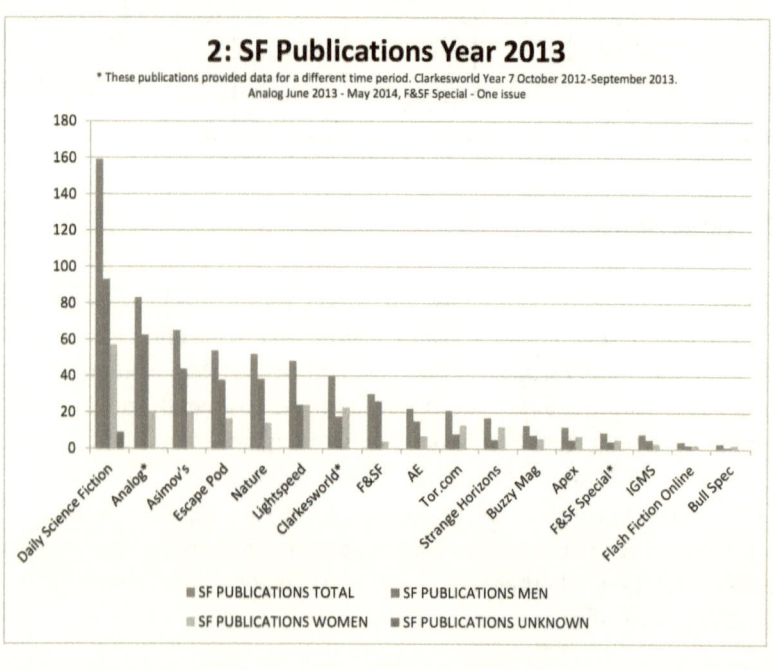

So, we cannot say that SFWA markets **in general** are skewed towards publishing stories by men. This does not mean there is no skew at all, rather it means that we cannot make broad generalizations about the group as a whole in this matter.

Indeed, we can see there are what seem to be large differences between **individual** markets, from *F&SF*'s ~80% of stories by men down to *Bull Spec*'s ~25% (see graph 3). Are these differences "significant?" Significant, in statistics, means that something is not just due to chance alone.

For example, if all of our markets published between 55% and 57% stories by men, we'd feel that this level of difference between the markets wasn't that important—we would feel comfortable making generalizations. If half of the SFWA qualifying markets published 95% stories by men, and half published only 7% stories by men, we'd be pretty sure that was an important difference! The difficulty is when the numbers aren't quite so clear-cut, such as those we have here. Thankfully, we have statistical tests to help us figure this out. It turns out that the differences we see here are significant, both for all stories and science fiction stories specifically.

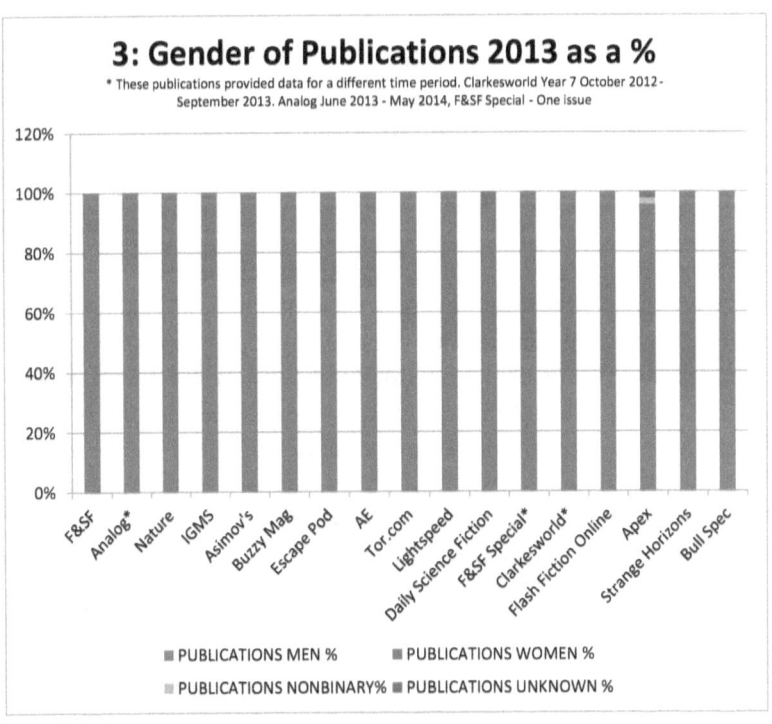

3: Gender of Publications 2013 as a %

* These publications provided data for a different time period. Clarkesworld Year 7 October 2012 - September 2013. Analog June 2013 - May 2014, F&SF Special - One issue

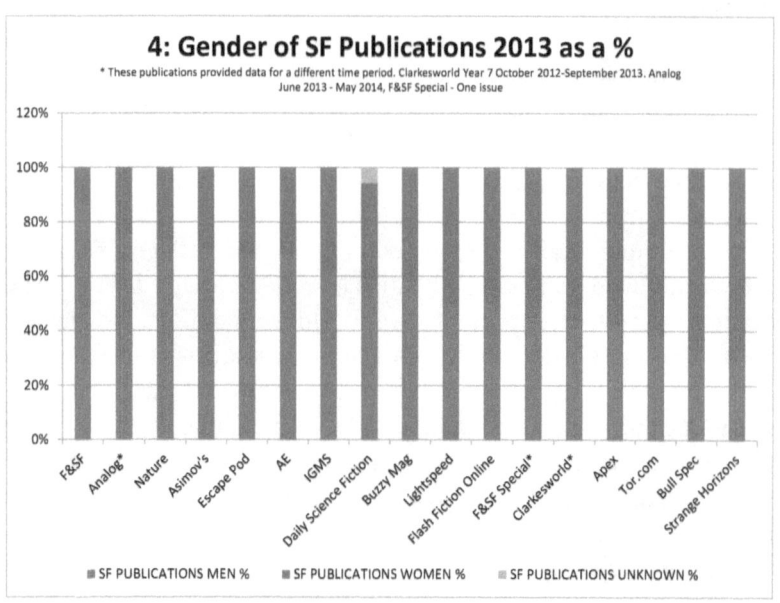

4: Gender of SF Publications 2013 as a %

* These publications provided data for a different time period. Clarkesworld Year 7 October 2012-September 2013. Analog June 2013 - May 2014, F&SF Special - One Issue

■ SF PUBLICATIONS MEN %   ■ SF PUBLICATIONS WOMEN %   ■ SF PUBLICATIONS UNKNOWN %

Enough markets skew towards authors who are women that we can't say anything about a possible gender bias of all sixteen markets as a group. So, where do the large differences we saw in **Publications Overall** come from? Well, for all stories, the markets that skew towards authors who are men averaged 71% stories by men, for a total of 328 publications, while those that skewed towards stories by women averaged 60% stories by women, for a total of 288.5 publications.

The markets that skew towards authors who are men averaged 67.5% science fiction stories by men, for a total of 329.5 science fiction publications, while those that skewed towards stories by women averaged 60.1% science fiction stories by women, for a total of 59.5 science fiction publications. From this, we can see that the markets that skew towards authors who are men publish more stories in total than those that skew towards authors who are women. Secondly, markets that skew towards authors who are men publish a higher proportion of stories by men than those that skew towards stories by women publish stories by women. (i.e., they have a greater degree of divergence from parity.) The overall result is more stories by men being published.

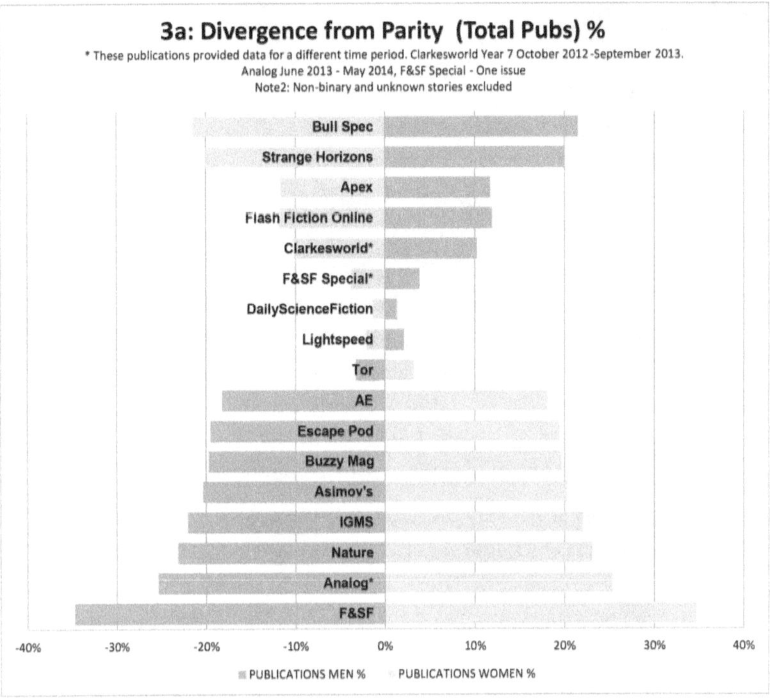

3a: Divergence from Parity (Total Pubs) %

* These publications provided data for a different time period. Clarkesworld Year 7 October 2012 -September 2013.
Analog June 2013 - May 2014, F&SF Special - One issue
Note2: Non-binary and unknown stories excluded

Categories (top to bottom): Bull Spec, Strange Horizons, Apex, Flash Fiction Online, Clarkesworld*, F&SF Special*, DailyScienceFiction, Lightspeed, Tor, AE, Escape Pod, Buzzy Mag, Asimov's, IGMS, Nature, Analog*, F&SF

Axis: -40%, -30%, -20%, -10%, 0%, 10%, 20%, 30%, 40%

■ PUBLICATIONS MEN %   PUBLICATIONS WOMEN %

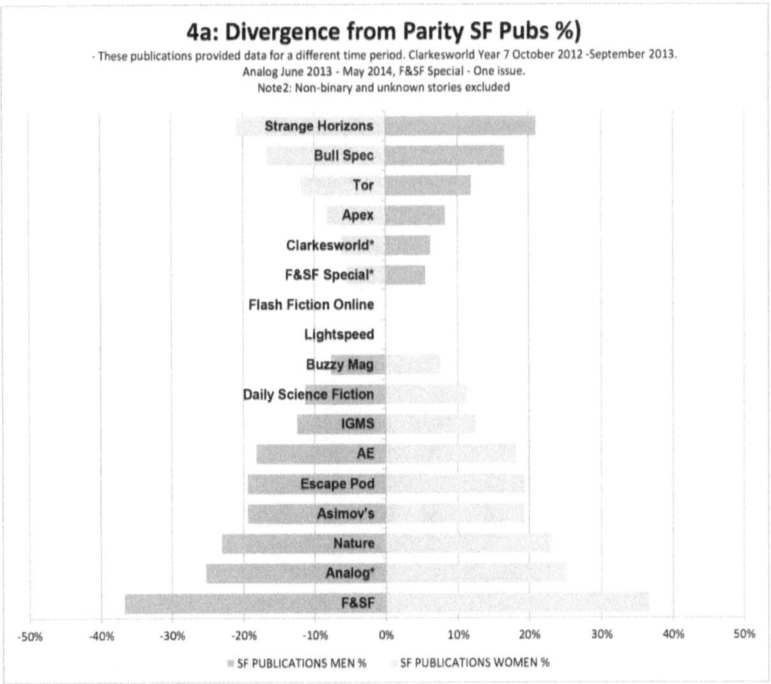

4a: Divergence from Parity SF Pubs %)

- These publications provided data for a different time period. Clarkesworld Year 7 October 2012 -September 2013.
Analog June 2013 - May 2014, F&SF Special - One issue.
Note2: Non-binary and unknown stories excluded

Categories (top to bottom): Strange Horizons, Bull Spec, Tor, Apex, Clarkesworld*, F&SF Special*, Flash Fiction Online, Lightspeed, Buzzy Mag, Daily Science Fiction, IGMS, AE, Escape Pod, Asimov's, Nature, Analog*, F&SF

Axis: -50%, -40%, -30%, -20%, -10%, 0%, 10%, 20%, 30%, 40%, 50%

■ SF PUBLICATIONS MEN %   SF PUBLICATIONS WOMEN %

Does Genre Matter?

Among the seventeen markets there are two intuitive categories: those that publish science-fiction-only, and those that publish science fiction in addition to other genres. Does this have an effect on the gender ratios of published science fiction stories? Are science fiction-only markets more likely to skew towards authors who are men than the science fiction sections of mixed-genre markets? If you've looked at the graphs, you'll see that it looks pretty likely. And indeed, according to the analysis, the answer is yes. Markets that publish science-fiction-only are correlated with a greater proportion of science fiction publications by men.

What about those markets that publish science fiction along with other genres? Their gender ratios tend to look like they're less skewed towards the side of stories by men, or in some cases, are skewed towards stories by women. However, when looking only at science fiction stories from these markets, these ratios change. By graphing science fiction stories as a percentage of total stories by men and women, we can see whether each gender is over-or under-represented in science fiction within each market, compared to their overall ratio. **So, for these markets, a high proportion of stories by men overall, does not** *necessarily* **mean a correspondingly high proportion of science fiction stories by men.**

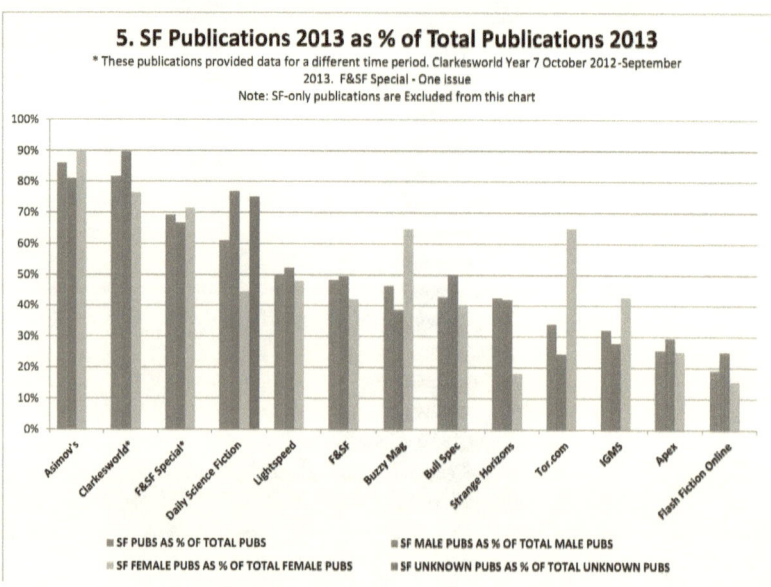

5. SF Publications 2013 as % of Total Publications 2013
* These publications provided data for a different time period. Clarkesworld Year 7 October 2012-September 2013. F&SF Special - One issue
Note: SF-only publications are Excluded from this chart

■ SF PUBS AS % OF TOTAL PUBS   ■ SF MALE PUBS AS % OF TOTAL MALE PUBS
■ SF FEMALE PUBS AS % OF TOTAL FEMALE PUBS   ■ SF UNKNOWN PUBS AS % OF TOTAL UNKNOWN PUBS

However, the fact that there is not an exact correspondence does not mean there is no relationship at all. Among these markets, the gender breakdown of total published stories *is* correlated with the gender breakdown of published science fiction stories. So, while *individual markets* may not display the exact same gender ratio for science fiction stories as for their overall stories, *markets in general* that tend to publish more men than women overall, also tend to publish more science fiction stories by men and vice-versa.

What About Editors?

During my research, two theories regarding gender representation of authors were brought to my attention.

The first theory: editors who are men might be more likely to select stories by men for publication, and editors who are women might be more likely to select stories by women for publication.

The second theory: older editors might be more likely to select stories by men for publication. (The reasoning behind this theory is that our tastes are shaped by our reading in early life, and that older editors are more likely to have grown up reading predominantly stories by men.)

I was unable to gather this data for all the editors and editorial teams, but with the data I did have, I tested those theories, with some interesting results.

As far as science fiction stories go, gender of senior editorial teams had no relationship with gender breakdown of published stories. (Here, "relationship" is another statistical term that means one thing depends on the other, or, affects or is affected by the other). However, when looking at total published stories in the markets, there *was* a relationship, with all-men senior editorial teams more likely to publish stories by men, when compared to all-woman senior editorial teams and mixed-gender senior editorial teams.

I also tested for relationships with the age of the senior editorial team. A very weak relationship was found, and only bears mentioning to maintain completeness in presentation.

What Does This All Mean?

There are a couple of takeaway points from the analysis so far.

If we believe that science fiction story authorship should reflect the gender breakdown of the world population, the analysis shows that currently, published science fiction short stories in SFWA qualifying markets are skewed towards authors who are men. However, this is not something that all markets contribute to equally. Multiple markets are close to parity, or even skew towards stories by women.

However, there's no one single factor that explains why some markets skew towards authors who are men and others skew towards authors who are women. While the science fiction-only markets all skew towards authors who are men, this characteristic can also be found in mixed-genre markets, especially when we look at science fiction stories separately.

Seven of the twelve mixed-genre markets have a greater representation of authors who are men in their science fiction section than in their overall catalogue. However, in general, mixed-genre markets that publish a high proportion of stories by women overall will also publish a high proportion of science fiction stories by women, and vice-versa.

This next bit is kind of fuzzy. Age of senior editorial team, while technically showing a relationship with a high representation of authors who are men, is not at a reliable result. Yes, there's a correlation, but it's very weak, such that we really can't draw any conclusions from it. Gender of senior editorial team does show a relationship with the gender breakdown of total published stories, but has no relationships with science fiction stories. This relationship with total stories, by the way, is a classic example of correlation vs. causation. We can't say that gender of senior editor *causes* the difference in gender representation in stories. It could be the other way around, or it could be due to a separate factor that affects both.

I mentioned at the beginning of this piece that publications are the end result of a process, and this analysis is a process as well. Looking at publications alone is insufficient. However, it does give us some important information—it shows us the situation as it is, and that's our first step in figuring out how it came to be.

Next time on Adventures in Statistics: Do Acceptances show the same patterns? Are editors displaying preferences in the stories they solicit and the reprints they choose to publish? Do different markets show significant differences in the gender ratios of submitted stories? Will our heroine have an Excel-induced meltdown?

Stay tuned . . .

ABOUT THE AUTHOR

Susan E. Connolly's short fiction and non-fiction have appeared in *Strange Horizons, Daily Science Fiction, The Center For Digital Ethics* and the fanzine *Journey Planet.* She is the author of *Damsel,* a middle-grade fantasy from

Mercier Press and *Granuaile,* an upcoming historical comic book from Atomic Diner. Her degree in Veterinary Medicine given her strong opinions about the accurate portrayal of animal sidekicks in fiction. Susan lives in Ireland, near the mountains. Also near the sea. Also near the forest (Ireland is a small country).

The Issue of Gender in Genre Fiction: The Math Behind it All

SUSAN E. CONNOLLY

Editor's Note: Knowing that some people will be curious about the math behind Susan's piece, we asked her to provide something a bit more technical for those more mathematically inclined among us.

Key Points for Understanding

- Publications refers to prose fiction published by a market, including reprints and solicited stories.
- Each publication is treated separately. Three publications by one market of stories by one author count as three separate data points for that category.
- Dual-authored stories by a man-woman team are considered as half a data point for each category.
- Serials are treated as follows:
  - Each installment is a separate data point for publications.
  - The series as a whole is one data point for acceptances.
- Not all markets provided full data in all categories, which meant they had to be excluded from some analyses, or have their data transformed. This is not ideal, but such cases are marked.
- No market in this study asks for authors to identify their gender when submitting. As such, this is not actually a study of science fiction publication and submission gender. Rather, it is a study of the *apparent gender* of submission authors based on:

- Use of gender-associated first names
- Use of gendered pronouns in public biographies
- Public information about gender identity
- The definition of "science fiction" is not easy. While some markets kept detailed data on science fiction vs. science fiction/fantasy vs. slipstream, most did not. As such, all such categories were considered as "science fiction."
- **Specific notes on individual markets regarding publications:**
  - *Lightspeed* operates a policy of gender parity in publications
  - *Buzzy Mag* operates as a continuous publication, with publications here those with a published date of 2013.
  - The *F&SF* Special Issue has not yet been published.

Market	Time Period	Data Verified by Editor	Genre
AE	Year 2013	Yes	Science fiction only
Analog	June 2013—May 2014	Yes	Science fiction only
Apex	Year 2013	No	Mixed genre
Asimov's	Year 2013	Yes	Mixed genre
Bull Spec	Year 2013	Yes	Mixed genre
Buzzy Mag	Year 2013	Yes	Mixed genre
Clarkesworld	Year 7 (October 2012-September 2013)	Yes	Mixed genre
Daily Science Fiction	Year 2013	Yes	Mixed genre
Escape Pod	Year 2013	Yes	Science fiction-only
F&SF	Year 2013	No	Mixed genre
F&SF Special Issue	July/August Special Issue	Yes	Mixed genre
Flash Fiction Online	Year 2013	Yes	Mixed genre
IGMS	Year 2013	Yes	Mixed genre
Lightspeed	Year 2013	Yes	Mixed genre
Nature	Year 2013	Yes	Science fiction only

Strange Horizons	Year 2013	Yes	Mixed genre
Tor.com	Year 2013	No	Mixed genre

A1: Publications by Gender1

Across seventeen markets, the total number of published stories was 996: 559.5 by men, 422.5 by women, 1 non-binary and 13 unknown.

The gender ratio was therefore 56.2% men, 42.4% women, 0.1% non-binary and 1.3% unknown.

Hypothesis: publications by men are equally likely as those by women to be above the median or not above the median.

Given a median of 50%, each market was assessed for whether its publications by men and publications by women were above or not above that median.

Median chi-square total publications			
Category	Authors who are men	Authors who are women	Total
Above median	9	7	16
not above median	8	10	18
Total	17	17	34

Results:
- chi square value: 0.472
- With a probability of 0.05 (or 95%) I have a critical value of 3.84.

Therefore I **cannot reject** our initial hypothesis.

Hypothesis: There are no significant differences in gender ratios relationship between markets.

To test this hypothesis, I performed a chi-square test between the variables of "market" and "gender ratio."

Results:
- chi sq: 92.65
- With a probability level of .001 (or 99.9%) our critical value is 39.25.

Therefore I can with confidence **reject** the hypothesis.

A2: Science Fiction Publications by Genderl

I performed the same tests for published science fiction stories.

Across seventeen markets, the total number of published science fiction stories was 649: 403 by men, 237 by women, 0 non-binary and 9 unknown.

The gender ratio was therefore 62.1% men, 36.5% women, 0% non-binary and 1.4% unknown.

Median chi-square science fiction publications			
Category	Authors who are men	Authors who are women	Total
Above median	9	6	15
Not above median	8	11	15
Total	15	15	30

Results:
- Our median chi square result was 1.07.

Therefore I **cannot reject** the null hypothesis.

Hypothesis: There are no significant differences in gender ratios relationship between markets for science fiction stories.

- Our chi-square result was 46.82.
- With a probability level of .001 (or 99.9%) our critical value is 39.25.

Therefore I can with confidence **reject** the null hypothesis.

A3: Science Fiction Story Publication Split by Genre of Market:l

Across four markets that published only science fiction, the total number of published science fiction stories was 253: 182 by men and 71 by women. This gives a gender ratio of 71.9% men, 28.1% women, 0% unknown.

Across thirteen markets that published other genres in addition to science fiction, the total number of published science fiction stories was 386: 213 by men, 164 by women and 9 unknown. This gives a gender ratio of 55.2% men, 42.5% women and 2.3% unknown.

Hypothesis: there is no correlation between a market publishing only science fiction, and a greater proportion of science fiction stories by men.

To assess this hypothesis, I used a point-biserial correlation. Our result was 0.54 (considered moderate).

Is this significant? I performed a T test for independent means to get a T-value of 2.46, with a P-value of 0.01. At the 95% probability for a one tailed t test the critical value is 1.753.

Therefore I can **reject** the null hypothesis.

A4: Non-Science_Fiction-Only Publications—Gender Split of Total Pubs vs. Gender Split of Science Fiction Pubsl

Using a Pearson's Correlation analysis I found an R value of 0.8863 (considered a strong positive correlation.)

So there is a tendency for markets which publish a high proportion of overall stories by men to publish a high proportion of science fiction stories by men (and vice-versa)

A5: Story Publication Split by Gender of Senior Editor

Note: One senior editor identifies as a genderqueer woman for political purposes and was included in the "woman" category for these assessments.

Across eight publications with men only as senior editor total stories published was 434, with 280 by men and 154 by women.

The gender ratio was therefore 64.52% men, 35.48% women.

Across five publications with women only as senior editor total stories published was 210, with 108.5 by men, 99.5 by women, 1 non-binary and 1 unknown.

The gender ratio was therefore 51.67% men, 47.38% women

Across four publications with mixed-gender editorial total stories published was 352 stories, with 171 by men, 169 by women, and 12 by unknown.

The gender ratio was therefore 48.58% men, 48.01% women and 3.41% unknown.

Hypothesis: Men-only senior editorial teams are not more likely to publish authors who are men.

I got a point-biserial correlation coefficient of 0.42, (considered moderate.)
I ran a T test for independent means to get a value of 1.80.
At the 95% probability for a one tailed t test the critical value is 1.75.

Therefore I **can reject** the null hypothesis.

A6: Science Fiction Story Publication Split by Gender of Senior Editorl

I performed the same tests for science fiction stories.
Across eight publications with men only as senior editors, total science fiction stories published was 320, with 210.5 by men and 109.5 by women.
The gender ratio was therefore 65.78% men, 34.22% women.
Across five publications with women only as senior editors, total science fiction stories published was 110, with 70.5 by men, 39.5 by women.
The gender ratio was therefore 64.1% men, 35.9% women.
Across four publications with mixed-gender editorial teams, total science fiction stories published was 205, with 117 by men, 79 by women, and 9 by unknown.
The gender ratio was therefore 57.07% men, 38.54% women and 4.39% unknown.

Hypothesis: Men-only senior editorial teams are not more likely to publish science fiction stories by men.

- Point biserial correlation coefficient—0.30 (moderate).
- Student t-test—1.21.
- At the 95% probability for a one tailed t test the critical value is 1.75.

Therefore, I **cannot reject** the null hypothesis.
Given the percentage difference, there may be a correlation between mixed-gender editorial teams and a smaller proportion of authors who are men.

Hypothesis: Single-gender senior editorial teams are not more likely to publish science fiction stories by men.

- Point biserial correlation coefficient—0.34 (moderate).
- Student t-test—1.42.
- At the 95% probability for a one tailed t test the critical value is 1.75.

Therefore, I **cannot reject** the null hypothesis.

A7: Story Publication Split by Average Age of Senior Editorial Team!

Four publications declined to provide age data: *Apex, Nature, Buzzy Mag, Tor.com*. This analysis used a Pearson's correlation.

Mean Age vs. Total Publications by Men %
The value of R is 0.3198. This is technically a positive correlation, but the relationship is weak.
The value of R2, the coefficient of determination, is 0.1023.

Mean Age vs. Science Fiction Publications by Men %
The value of R is -0.0082. This is technically a negative correlation, but the relationship is weak.
The value of R2, the coefficient of determination, is 0.0001.

Median Age vs. Total Publications by Men %
The value of R is 0.3281. This is technically a positive correlation, but the relationship is weak.
The value of R2, the coefficient of determination, is 0.1076.

Median Age vs. Science Fiction Publications by Men %
The value of R is -0.0036. This is technically a positive correlation, but the relationship is weak.
The value of R2, the coefficient of determination, is 0.

ABOUT THE AUTHOR

Susan E. Connolly's short fiction and non-fiction have appeared in *Strange Horizons, Daily Science Fiction, The Center For Digital Ethics* and the fanzine *Journey Planet*. She is the author of *Damsel*, a middle-grade fantasy from Mercier Press and *Granuaile*, an upcoming historical comic book from Atomic Diner. Her degree in Veterinary Medicine given her strong opinions about the accurate portrayal of animal sidekicks in fiction. Susan lives in Ireland, near the mountains. Also near the sea. Also near the forest (Ireland is a small country).

Wendig's Golden Prolific: A Conversation with Chuck Wendig

ALVARO ZINOS-AMARO

Chuck Wendig is the author of the published novels *Blackbirds, Mockingbird, The Cormorant, Under the Empyrean Sky, Blue Blazes, Double Dead, Bait Dog, Dinocalypse Now, Beyond Dinocalypse* and *Gods & Monsters: Unclean Spirits.*

He is co-writer of the short film *Pandemic*, the feature film *HiM*, and the Emmy-nominated digital narrative *Collapsus*. Wendig has contributed over two million words to the game industry. He is also well known for his profane-yet-practical advice to writers, which he dispenses at his blog, terribleminds.com, and through several popular e-books, including *The Kick-Ass Writer*, published by Writers Digest.

I had the pleasure of chatting with him about corn-punk, Pac-Man, muse elves, and the shedding of literary illusions regarding the novel.

By now it's well-known that you're a prolific writer, but I've heard you mention that when you were writing Blackbirds *(2012), the first Miriam Black novel, you were unable to finish it for four years. What were some of the key things that you learned during that time?*

I often refer to myself as a pantser by heart but a plotter by necessity, so when someone taught me how to outline—well, not really taught me so much as just forced me to sit down and do it—it was pretty amazing how suddenly I was able to get all the ducks that had previously been wandering akimbo in one neat little duck row.

I had this idea that the outline killed magic. And I understand the point, and people still say to me, "When I write the outline, it's not fun. It doesn't feel like I'm originating the story anymore. I'm not harnessing magic so much as I'm just writing details." Which I understand, and I think some people can over-outline, and kill their own enthusiasm about a book by getting down to every beat. But I think if you hit the tent-pole pieces, the broad bases, the magic is still there. Planning a journey from point A to point B, whether you're walking it, or doing in a car, or doing it in a story, you're always free, upon execution of the journey, to make changes, and take exits you didn't think you would normally take. And that's where the magic still exists.

Part of it was also just about shedding some of the illusions I had about writing novels. I had already gotten rid of some of those illusions, because before that novel I was a freelance writer for the pen-and-paper game industry, so I was very good with discipline and deadlines, which are necessary for a writing career. But somehow I still held the novel as this artistic pinnacle, this thing that was very high up and required all these artful things. Losing that illusion was valuable to me.

Now that you do follow a more structured approach, do you find that your characters still surprise you?

It's one of those things where I'm aware that I control the characters. I'm not under the illusion that they're mysterious entities from beyond space and time who puppet me, and I'm just their machine. Sometimes we have this idea—and it's a cool idea—that we're like a conduit for the characters, a prophet for them in some way. But I think what happens is that you have to let your conscious and sub-conscious minds have a little field day.

The stuff in the outline is stuff you've thought about more completely in the front of your brain. But then there's all the stuff that goes in the back of your brain, stuff that happens in the life you live, stuff you've seen, experienced, things that happen when you sleep. Your brain is like a slow cooker when you sleep, and all kinds of weird ideas bubble up.

So for a lot of that, you just have to have the opportunity for it to come out. You can't be so married to an outline that you're not willing to seize those moments of inspiration. But again, it's important to see that those moments of inspiration are not externally driven. There's not some little muse elf under my desk quietly feeding me Post-it notes when I've appeased him well. It's all me. We're our own gods in this world: we just have to listen to all the weird, secret, unconscious/sub-conscious language.

Given that your earlier works are horror- or crime-centric, what led you to YA science fiction with the *Heartland* trilogy?

It started with a joke. I was just kidding around on my blog. I do flash fiction challenges and talk a lot about writing and genre. I was talking about "-punk", like cyber-punk, diesel-punk, steam-punk, and I wanted to create new types, so as an example I came up with "corn-punk." It's about a world taken over by corn, and the rich people control it, and the poor people tend to it.

And then I thought about it and said, "Dibs, you can't have that" but I still put it in the post and waved everybody away, and made it clear it was mine by urinating on it or however it is you mark things. That was the seed of the idea. It wasn't really a story or a book yet, but the core, or kernel—pun—of an idea. It was around that time I discovered that my wife was pregnant.

Talk about a kernel!

Right. Talk about a seedling. So I realized that my books up until this point had really put the "adult" in "adult fiction," and since I wouldn't want my son to read them until he was at least thirty-five or thirty-six years old, I thought, "Let's get a little closer to his age and meet him halfway." Now when he's maybe fourteen or fifteen I'll have a book for him.

Did you find that your approach had to change because it was science fiction?

Yes, because it requires a lot more worldbuilding. I spent a lot more time not just on worldbuilding but on the draft in general. Previous to that, while *Blackbirds* took four or five years of being lost in the wilderness like old people get lost in the mall, *Mockingbird* (2012) I wrote in thirty days, *The Cormorant* (2013) in forty-five. There wasn't a ton of worldbuilding there. I was very comfortable and confident in what I was doing.

The first *Heartland* book took me about a year. I still wrote the first draft in about two months, and literally finished it the week my son was born, but it still took a year after that to draft and redraft. By the end of that probably half of the book was entirely rewritten. I was trying to make sure all the worldbuilding didn't overwhelm the story. You still have to tell a story about people doing awesome things, you can't be like, "Here's a detail about corn." So it was all about finding the balance and managing it.

You were setting out to write the *Dune* of corn.

Yes, corn-*Dune*! Actually, John Hornor Jacobs, who has written his own wonderful YA with *The Twelve-Fingered Boy* series, blurbed it as "Star Wars meets John Steinbeck." That's one of my favorite descriptions.

Can you share anything about what we can expect in volumes two and three of the *Heartland* trilogy?

Sure. I'm writing three now, so I won't go too deep into that one. But *Blightborn*, the second book, which comes out in July, is almost twice the size of the first book. Not only is it more epic in scope, it takes us up into the skies, into the flotillas, and it focuses more heavily on Gwennie, in addition to Cael. About half the book is from Gwennie's perspective and it shifts perspective a lot more. There's more worldbuilding details in this one: more about the history of the Empyrean, the religion and so on. It's much meatier. The third one will probably be slimmer again, more like the summation at the end of a standoff.

Given the book's preoccupation with genetically-engineered corn, I'm interested in whether you watch documentaries like *Food Inc.* or *Fed Up*, and if you monitor your own consumption of corn/ corn-derivatives in your diet?

Yep. *King Corn* is a good one. All of that stuff informs the book.

And yes, we do, not because I'm somehow heavily anti-GMO, but because I'm anti the power behind GMOs. I don't like any one thing in concentrated corporate power. Specially now, having a son, we're more aware of what goes into his mouth, as well as mine, so we try to keep to things that are not highly processed. I don't worry too much about fats, and even to some degree sugars, as long as they're natural and not over-wrought, but it's tricky. It's amazing how many things are made of corn.

Do you have a career plan for the next few years?

It's very much about options for me. If I want to write X, Y, Z books and those books aren't selling, what do I do? If for some reason a certain publisher or market falls apart, what do I do? I'm frequently telling people on my blog that you need to cleave to diversification in your work. You can't just publish one way with one company with one genre and expect to be safe. You might be, by the grace of all of the gods and that little elf under your desk, but if for some reason that all breaks apart like a cookie under a foot, you have to wonder where you're going to jump to next. If you have already diversified, you have ways to move that don't feel artificial, to you or to your audience. That's the key for me: being diversified.

What's the worst writing advice (besides "Quit") that you've ever been given?

I went to school and I focused on fiction writing in English. There were two schools of thought. My actual advisor and the teacher who I worked most with was literarily-minded but very genre-friendly. You could sit and talk with him about *Fantastic Four* or *Hulk* comic books. There was another teacher who was a poet laureate, and anytime you tried to write something for her class that was genre-based she would say, "Stay away from genre." I don't think all literary writers are like that, but certainly in academia you find a little of that.

Given that I make my money from writing genre fiction, and from what I understand she does not make money from writing, except teaching writing, I'm going to go with that genre writing was a pretty good choice for me.

Do you gleefully send her a signed copy of each new novel you publish, with a few dollar bills tucked inside the pages for good measure?

I should do that. Here's a couple of bucks: enjoy your poems.
Wow, that would be such a jerk move. But so tempting.

Last question: Any chance that we'll ever get to see a re-tooled version of the buddy-up adventure between Pac-Man and the Xenomorphs from *Alien* you thought up when you were a kid?

If I could get the rights to those stories, if someone were to allow me to write a licensed comic book featuring Pac-Man vs. the Xenomorphs, I would be on that like flies on a dead body.

ABOUT THE AUTHOR

Alvaro is the co-author, with Robert Silverberg, of *When the Blue Shift Comes,* which received a starred review from *Library Journal.* Alvaro's short fiction and poetry have appeared or are forthcoming in *Analog, Nature, Galaxy's Edge, Apex* and other venues, and Alvaro was nominated for the 2013 Rhysling Award. Alvaro's reviews, critical essays and interviews have appeared in *The Los Angeles Review of Books, Strange Horizons, SF Signal, The New York Review of Science Fiction, Foundation,* and other markets. Alvaro currently edits the blog for *Locus.*

Another Word: Chasing the High

DANIEL ABRAHAM

When you start out wanting to be a writer, you're screwed. You haven't read enough to really understand what writing is. There are all sorts of different genres, and you may not know if you're better at detective novels or literary vignettes or personal essays. You're pretty impressed by some of the stuff you've done when you're noodling around, but most of it's not very good. (And you're probably not actually sure which parts are impressive and which ones aren't very good.) There's a whole obscure mechanism between you and getting publishing that you've got **no** idea about, and you don't want to look stupid. Plus, it seems like everyone you know wants to be a writer, and almost all of them fail, which is, let's say, *discouraging*. The sheer volume of things you need to figure out is unmanageable and huge. You're screwed.

When you start sending out stories, you're screwed. There are only a few markets that publish the kind of stories you write, and the slush piles there are like broken faucets that won't turn off. You want to stand out, but short of printing your story on bright blue paper or including a chocolate bar with the submission, you don't know how to do that. No one knows your name.

Every rejection slip—and holy cow are there a lot of rejection slips—makes it a little easier to just not send out the next story. The idea of paying someone to publish your stuff just so it's out there—just so you can see your words in print—starts to seem like maybe a pretty good idea even though part of you knows that's the despair talking. The Holy Grail is a personal rejection letter, because at least that would mean someone cared enough to respond to you. You're screwed.

When you start selling a few stories, you're kind of screwed. You have a few things in print, and you've gotten checks for a couple hundred dollars to prove it! The people in your writer's group threw you a little party after the first one, but when the third sale came through, the congratulations started getting kind of perfunctory.

Now that you don't need the emotional support, you're not getting as much of it. Except that you're still basically unknown, and you're still getting an awful lot of rejections that sting just as much as they did before. You've sent your novel out to a few agents and gotten polite "Not for me" answers. You've gone to a few conventions and actually been on panels, which on one hand was really cool, and on the other left you feeling kind of like an impostor. The world's full of people who published a few short stories and then vanished without a literary trace, and you're starting to think that you may be one of those.

When you sell your first novel, you're screwed, but only a *little*. Yeah, there are still a lot of dangers and hurdles coming. The book may or may not get good reviews. You don't know how it's going to sell. You're really jazzed by the cover art, even if there are maybe a couple little things you'd have done differently. Your friends and family are congratulating you. There's the anxiety that maybe it will fail, but when you walk into the bookstore and see your book on the shelf for the first time, it's like being in a dream. Yes, if the numbers aren't good, the publisher may not pick up the next book. Yes, the advance you got for it was less than you'd have made working a minimum wage job for the same hours you spent writing. Yes, some of your unpublished friends seem a little resentful. But at least now you can say you're really a writer. This is kind of the high-water mark. You should enjoy it.

When you've sold a few books, you're screwed. Your first novel didn't set the world on fire, but it did okay. It sold through maybe eighty percent of the copies that went out. Only then the bookstores ordered twenty percent fewer of the next title, and that one sold through about eighty percent. So when the third book hit, and they ordered eighty percent of eighty percent of your first book's numbers, you started looking at a consistent pattern of lower sales, and the eBook sales haven't been high enough to buck the trend.

Now your editor is talking about how the subgenre you write in is kind of oversaturated. And there was that one asshole reviewer on Goodreads who totally savaged you for no good reason. When you very politely pointed out that they'd misread the book, the Internet fell on your head for a week. You're in the death spiral. The good reviews you get are easy to forget and the bad ones linger at the back of your head for days. You're watching your career die, and the war stories from other writers about the times their careers were shot out from under them only help a little. You're screwed.

When you hit the bestsellers list, you're screwed, and no one believes it. You're a success *fercrissakes*! This is what the brass ring looks like. Your series actually built, you've quit your day job. You're supporting yourself on the writing alone. You don't get to complain anymore. *Ever.* Because nobody has any sympathy.

Someone wrote a savage blog post that got passed around dissecting how exactly your books show you're a vacuous, stupid, venal person who wants to degrade all that's good in the world because you're stupid. And then a hundred comments after it praised the blogger for being brave enough to speak the truth.

A reviewer at a major magazine uses your name as a synonym for bad writing? Suck it up. Or stay off the Internet. If you defend yourself, you're only going to make it worse. And the sneaking suspicion that you're only selling your story to the anthology so they can put your name on the cover (and not because the story is good) isn't something anyone wants to hear. The way that your new book coming out has gone from a massive rush to "Yay, now get back to work" isn't interesting. Your problems don't count anymore. You won!

If that's a little lonely, a little isolating, less fun than you thought it was going to be, if you still feel like an impostor, literally nobody wants to hear you whine about it. So shut up and live the dream. No one wants to hear how you're screwed.

When you're one of the handful that make it all the way to the top—recognition, awards, more money than you'll ever be able to spend—weirdly, you're screwed. You're a celebrity now. When you go out in public, strangers come up to you constantly and it's your job to be nice and polite no matter how awkward it is or how bad you feel.

If you make a bad joke on Twitter, it's a headline on *Slate* and *Gawker*. The praise for your work seems almost unrelated to the actual words you put on the page, and the story about who you are feels like people are talking about someone else.

Whenever you meet new people, it feels like they can't see past your persona. There are maybe three or four people in your life who aren't asking for things from you. The money is great, and it solves a lot of problems, but not all of them. They won't let you walk the floor at Comicon anymore because of the security risk. You don't go out to the movies. You know that your writing is a commodity now just because it's got your name on it.

The jokes about how you could blow your nose on a piece of paper and get a six-figure advance are funny because they speak to a real fear. Maybe you're not good anymore, because you don't have to be. The passion that started you down this path is still there, and so is the fear. You want to be good, but maybe you're *only* successful. And with the story about you so much bigger than the story you're writing, there may not be a way to judge anymore.

A writing career is a constantly shifting environment where there is no promised land. There's only a changing, and hopefully improving, set of problems.

The constants—the pleasure of reading a really good story or paragraph or sentence or phrase (or, even better, writing it), the well-considered praise of a respected voice, the sense of having learned something new or relearned something old in a deeper way—have to be enough, because they're what we have.

Sufficient unto the day is the evil thereof. And the good. And the work.

ABOUT THE AUTHOR

Daniel Abraham is a writer of genre fiction with a dozen books in print and over thirty published short stories. His work has been nominated for the Nebula, World Fantasy, and Hugo Awards and has been awarded the International Horror Guild Award. He also writes as MLN Hanover and (with Ty Franck) as James S. A. Corey. He lives in the American Southwest.

Editor's Desk:
Clearing Something Off My Desk
NEIL CLARKE

When we launched *Clarkesworld*, we had every intention of releasing an annual anthology that collected all of the original stories published that year. The first two, *Realms 1* and *Realms 2*, were published on-schedule, but things crashed to a halt at volume three. Part of the problem was financial and the rest was me.

After my heart attack nearly two years ago, I refocused my efforts in making *Clarkesworld* a full-time career and mapped out how to get there. One of the items on that list was to catch up on our languishing print anthologies and issues, so I dedicated some of my sitting-on-the-couch recovery time to learning InDesign and book design.

By February of the next year, I had managed to publish several back issues in print and the first of many long-overdue anthologies, *Clarkesworld: Year Three*. By the end of the year, I was regularly producing print editions of each new issue, had completed working backwards to issue fifty, and published two more anthologies: *Clarkesworld: Year Four* and *Clarkesworld: Year Five*.

For the first part of this year, I've placed an emphasis on getting completely caught up with the anthologies. After that, I'll go back and tackle issues one through forty-nine. Moving ever closer to that goal, I published our largest volume, *Clarkesworld: Year Six*, in late May. Like earlier volumes, *Year Six* features cover art from a prior issue of the magazine. This time it's "Space Journey" by Martin Faragasso, which originally appeared on issue seventy-one. The stories are from issues sixty-one through seventy-two, which coincidentally is the year of my heart attack. It's somewhat sobering to realize that everything from that point forward has been done on time I almost didn't get. Anyhow, I'm quite proud of this volume.

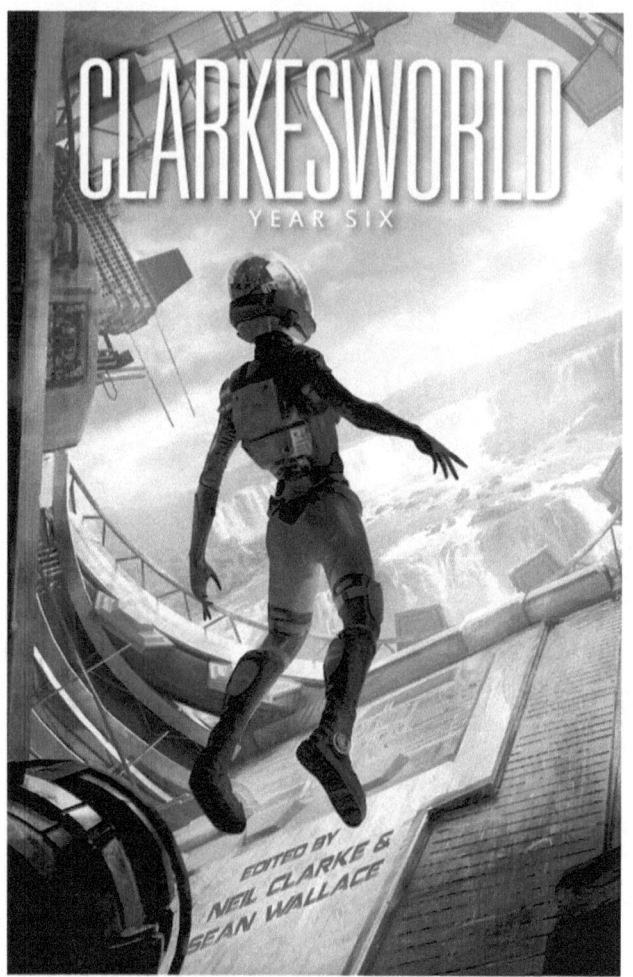

Contents:

This volume brings me close, but not quite up to date. I have one more volume to finish before October triggers the next one. Wish me luck!

If you'd like to purchase any of our anthologies in trade paperback or ebook editions, they can be ordered direct from us, via Wyrm Publishing, or from any of the booksellers listed on our site.

ABOUT THE AUTHOR

Neil Clarke is the editor of *Clarkesworld Magazine,* owner of Wyrm Publishing and a current Hugo Award Nominee for Best Editor (short form). He currently lives in NJ with his wife and two children.

About the Artists
ARTUR FAST AND KEMANE BA

Artur Fast is a Kazakhstani artist currently living in Bochum, Germany. He has been a freelance artist for eight years and a concept artist for Flare Games for the last four. He is also part of LMBN, a poetry slam show, in which he creates livepaintings. His current focus is on walls and street art.

WEBSITE

drawcrowd.com/arturfast

Kemane Ba is a freelance illustrator/animator in Frankfurt.

WEBSITE

drawcrowd.com/kemanski